FOUR CALLING BIRDS

Twelve Days of Christmas

Emily E K Murdoch

ARE YOU SIGNED UP FOR DRAGONBLADE'S BLOG?

You'll get the latest news and information on exclusive giveaways, exclusive excerpts, coming releases, sales, free books, cover reveals and more.

Check out our complete list of authors, too!

No spam, no junk. That's a promise!

Sign Up Here

www.dragonbladepublishing.com

Dearest Reader;

Thank you for your support of a small press. At Dragonblade Publishing, we strive to bring you the highest quality Historical Romance from some of the best authors in the business. Without your support, there is no 'us', so we sincerely hope you adore these stories and find some new favorite authors along the way.

Happy Reading!

CEO, *Dragonblade Publishing*

Additional Dragonblade books by Author Emily E K Murdoch

Twelve Days of Christmas
Twelve Drummers Drumming
Eleven Pipers Piping
Ten Lords a Leaping
Nine Ladies Dancing
Eight Maids a Milking
Seven Swans a Swimming
Six Geese a Laying
Five Gold Rings
Four Calling Birds

The De Petras Saga
The Misplaced Husband (Book 1)
The Impoverished Dowry (Book 2)
The Contrary Debutante (Book 3)
The Determined Mistress (Book 4)
The Convenient Engagement (Book 5)

The Governess Bureau Series
A Governess of Great Talents (Book 1)
A Governess of Discretion (Book 2)
A Governess of Many Languages (Book 3)
A Governess of Prodigious Skill (Book 4)
A Governess of Unusual Experience (Book 5)
A Governess of Wise Years (Book 6)
A Governess of No Fear (Novella)

Never The Bride Series
Always the Bridesmaid (Book 1)
Always the Chaperone (Book 2)
Always the Courtesan (Book 3)

Always the Best Friend (Book 4)
Always the Wallflower (Book 5)
Always the Bluestocking (Book 6)
Always the Rival (Book 7)
Always the Matchmaker (Book 8)
Always the Widow (Book 9)
Always the Rebel (Book 10)
Always the Mistress (Book 11)
Always the Second Choice (Book 12)
Always the Mistletoe (Novella)
Always the Reverend (Novella)

The Lyon's Den Series
Always the Lyon Tamer

Pirates of Britannia Series
Always the High Seas

De Wolfe Pack: The Series
Whirlwind with a Wolfe

Selina and Arthur and Dorothea
Caroline
Arabella
Sophia
Esther
Lucy
Jemima
London
Rupert and Frances
Joy
Harmony
William and Leonora
Olivia
Katarina
Isabella
Maria
Bath
Chalcroft
Fitzroy

CHAPTER ONE

IF LUCY WAS not careful, she was going to lose her temper—certainly not something she should do this close to Christmas.

Still. Her sister Esther was pushing her to the edge.

"Esther!"

Esther dropped the gloves she was supposed to be wrapping as a Christmas gift for their mother to the floor, she jumped at Lucy's shout. "Goodness, what?"

Lucy shook her head. It was remarkable. Esther was only a few years older than her, and they had been raised together, growing closer as they grew older. But this December, something had been different. Something strange.

Though it had been Esther's idea to set up the dining room to wrap Christmas gifts, she had done naught but sit, gaze drifting off into the distance. It was enough to drive one to distraction.

Lucy rolled her eyes. "I have been attempting to get your attention for nigh on a full minute. Are you sure you are feeling well?"

She had not precisely examined her sister until now, but now she looked closely, Esther did look rather…different.

The same fiery red hair, the same blue eyes, it was always obvious to strangers that the two Fitzroy ladies were sisters; but Lucy could see a pallor in Esther that was unusual.

Lucy frowned, considering whether to say anything. Esther

was unlike Jemima, their eldest sister, all prickles and stings, therefore unlikely to get upset at being questioned.

But still—she had been acting strangely for days now. It was most unaccountable.

"Lucy," said Esther quietly, retrieving the gloves from the floor, "have you ever…well. Kissed a gentleman?"

Lucy's eyes widened. "What?"

What sort of question was that! True, three of their sisters were married, and Caroline certainly did not stop going on about how wonderful her husband was—something Lucy had attempted to tease out of her, to no avail.

The very idea of Lucy merely accepting the first gentleman who asked her—not that anyone had. Balls, dances, card parties…they offered so little in the way of diversion.

"I am just curious," Esther said hastily, her attention drifting away from her sister once more. "One hears such stories…"

Lucy stared. *What on earth had got into her?*

This was supposed to be a normal, calm, Fitzroy Christmas—none of the scandalous proposals that previous Christmases had featured. Even Sophia, the youngest Fitzroy, was excited about the Christmas festivities this year.

So why on earth was Esther so fixated on…on kissing gentlemen?

"One hears such stories…"

"One does indeed," said Lucy with a growing smile. *Well, if this was the conversational topic that would awaken Esther…* "Why, I actually saw Miss Tilbury just the other week! She was dressed so fine, Esther, you could not imagine, and I heard she has taken not one, but two gentlemen as her lovers!"

Esther nodded, pulling a ream of brown paper toward her. "Yes, yes, good."

"Good?"

"I mean," she said, "good of you to tell me. But if a gentleman kissed you, Lucy…what would you do?"

There was something very odd going on here; and Lucy

could not entirely tell what it was. It certainly could not be anything to do with the Duke of Kendal, that gentleman Esther had walked out with once last week. Or was it the week before?

"I do not think a proper gentleman would kiss me, unless he asked permission to do so," said Lucy slowly, wrinkling her nose.

Well, honestly! The thought of a man just…just taking that sort of liberty and without any respect! It was unconscionable!

It reminded her of something Percy said once.

At the thought of her closest friend, the tension in Lucy's forehead disappeared and she grinned, unable to help herself. She knew precisely what old Ardingley would say about such a thing!

"Percy once said it was only rebellious girls who kissed gentlemen they had no intention of marrying," Lucy said with a laugh. "He was so funny, actually—we were talking about—"

"Yes, well," interrupted Esther. "But what do you think? If a gentleman kissed you, do you think he had more serious intentions? Marriage, I mean?"

Marriage? Goodness, her sister was rather serious—but then, matrimony was rather a serious business.

At least, it would be. It was not that Lucy had never considered such a thing. It was more that it happened to other people. To her sisters, to her cousins. Not to her.

Visited by a hilarious memory, Lucy giggled. "Percy kissed me once, do you remember? Yes, he leaned forward most unexpectedly this summer at the fair we attended?" Lucy laughed. "My word, I did chortle at the time, and he laughed, too, and said what a marvelous jest it was. Do you remember?"

Esther nodded, but she did not appear at all diverted. To the contrary, her face fell, and her gaze shifted to the terribly knitted gloves she would be giving their mother for Christmas. Lucy had offered to help with the casting off, but Esther would do it herself, albeit poorly.

Lucy's laughter died away, but she could not help but finish the story. "It really was rather strange, and when I asked Percy later precisely what he meant by such a thing, he laughed away quite merrily and said I was not to take such things to heart, and I must say I have not thought of it since then."

That was the wonderful thing about Percy, Lucy thought as warmth soared into her stomach. The young man—more a boy, at the time—had befriended the Fitzroy family nearly a decade and a half ago, when they were children.

It was odd to think of a world without Percy. Lucy could not recall such a time; the man—a dashing gentleman, she sup-posed—was such an important feature in her life, it could not be comprehended without him.

Of all the Fitzroy sisters, and there were plenty of them, it was she who had become his particular friend. Who spent summers racing through the parks of London and winters marveling at its coffeehouses. Who shared his call.

Lucy's gaze sharpened as her mind prodded her about the topic of their conversation. Kissing.

What on earth had Esther been doing?

"But why do you ask?" said Lucy suddenly, frowning. "All this about kissing—have…have you…"

The question went unfinished but it did not need to be. Lucy's mouth fell open.

No. It was not possible; *not calm, quiet, Esther!*

If there was going to be a scandal in the family, a real one, why then Lucy absolutely had to know all of it. Was it the Duke of Kendal? Who else could it be?

"It was just one kiss."

"Who?" demanded Lucy, present wrapping entirely forgot-ten. "Goodness, Esther, no wonder you have been so distracted all day—in all haste, tell me who!"

"It is just…a gentleman," said Esther wretchedly, still not meeting her gaze.

It was perhaps the most exciting thing that had happened all year, and Lucy leaned forward eagerly to hear all the details. This was marvelous! A Christmas romance, absolutely perfect. Percy would be absolutely agog to hear all about it.

"A gentleman?"

Esther nodded. "He is…well, I believe he is interested in marrying me for my fortune."

Oh, of all the boring, dull, irritating, things… "Oh."

It was such a shame. Lucy had such high hopes for a scandal—well, not precisely a scandal, but an intrigue. A romance, a true romance. A handsome gentleman sweeping her sister off her feet, suddenly declaring his love for her, riding off into the sunset…

It was all too good to be true.

"But then I thought, if I could make him care for me, truly care for me, then it would be as though it were a love match, do you see?" Esther said eagerly. "And I thought for a while he was starting to care for me…at least, he kissed me, and is that not half of the battle? For he would not have kissed me if he did not care for me, if he were not considering…"

Lucy turned to the table, heart sinking. It was the same, dull story all over again. An aloof gentleman attempting to marry a Fitzroy fortune. How many times had Esther told her of such boring men, attempting to charm their father without even bothering to make her sister smile?

Why, Percy had said before that he thought it ridiculous the Fitzroy sisters did not look a little closer for husbands, and Lucy quite agreed. Caroline had married her childhood sweetheart, had she not?

Sudden silence. She looked up to see Esther looking at her expectantly, and Lucy swallowed. She had not precisely been paying attention—but then, she had heard the tone of her sister's words, and she had sounded excited.

Lucy nodded with a smile. "Good. That's good."

A little closer for husbands…

Those had been Percy's words, and Lucy had never considered them before, at least, not properly. He had mentioned it at a card party they had all been invited to—one of Lady Romeril's dreaded affairs, and he had looked…well, most strange when he had said them.

The normally perennial grin had been absent; the smile she knew so well entirely gone. Why, he had almost been serious. What on earth had he meant by it?

"Lucy. Lucy!"

It made no sense—but then, there had been other times Percy had been nonsensical, hadn't there? The memory of that strange kiss returned to Lucy's mind, her mind raising it as though it was connected. The warmth of his hand on hers, the proximity of a gentleman who had only ever remained a respectful distance away.

The strange tug of her stomach, the way the earth had spun a little just afterward. It had been quick, warm, and welcoming, yet entirely unexpected. And then she had laughed. Well, what had Percy expected her to do?

"Just a joke, he said," Lucy said vaguely. "And yet…when I look back—"

"There you two are!"

Both Esther and Lucy quickly scrabbled to hide the Christmas gifts as yet unwrapped.

"Papa!" Esther exclaimed as their father hastily put a hand over his eyes as he stood in the doorway. "You know you were not supposed to come in here!"

"I forgot, a terrible crime!" said their Papa with a laugh. "I only came to deliver the post, good ladies, please do not poke my eyes out!"

Lucy rolled her eyes as she giggled, getting up and pulling the letter from her father's hand. "You really are very silly, Papa."

"Undoubtedly so," said Arthur cheerfully. "I shall leave you to it, ladies."

Shutting the door behind him, Lucy was relieved to hear her sister giggle. At least she was not completely absorbed by this strange gentleman who had the audacity to wish to marry her only for her fortune.

The very idea!

Her gaze dropped to the letter in her hands, her heart soaring—but it immediately returned to earth as she saw the addressee.

"It's for you," said Lucy heavily as she sat back at the table. "I thought it might have been from—"

"Percy," Esther chimed in. "What, you think I could not guess that?"

Lucy handed over the letter with a sigh, then returned to her wrapping. Yes, it was too much to expect it would be from Percy. That was the trouble with one's best friend being a gentleman, and not a lady—other than Esther, of course.

Gentlemen always had something to do, things of great import. Places to go, people to visit. All she had to do was wait at home for invitations. It was most irritating. Why, Percy had been out of town most of the autumn, only returning at the beginning of December for the Christmas period. They had shared many walks together to make up for it.

Lucy's gaze flickered over to Esther, and saw with astonishment that her sister's cheeks had flamed into scarlet. "Who's it from?"

Esther looked up hastily. "No one. Arabella."

Arabella? Their sister who was spending Christmas in Bath, with her husband? Why on earth would she be writing to Esther, and not all of them?

For a moment, Lucy was tempted to ask why on earth she said it was from no one—but there was such an odd look on Esther's face that she decided against it. What her sister wished to do was her affair, and she saw no point in getting involved.

She would hear all about it in the end, she was sure. Until then, Esther had to be left to her own devices; it was the only way to deal with her.

Besides, it was hard not to be piqued Arabella had not written to all of them. The entire London branch of the Fitzroy family wished to hear the Bath family gossip.

"Of course, she would write to you," said Lucy with a wry

smile. "Tell me about it later, I am going to attempt this ribbon."

Christmas gifts were all very well, she thought, and they were pleasant enough to choose and purchase—but when it came to wrapping the things, they were most trying. Lucy could never get the ribbons to behave, something Sophia excelled at.

As Esther broke the seal of their sister's letter, Lucy wondered whether it was worth hunting out Sophia and asking for her assistance. At least, for all the gifts save those for her, naturally.

What had their sister Sophia said she was doing today? Was she at home, or—

A sudden crash—Lucy looked up, startled, to see Esther had risen to her feet, her face a beetroot red, her chair tipped over.

"I will read it upstairs," she babbled without looking at her sister.

"Esther, are you feeling unwell?" asked Lucy hurriedly, rising in turn but receiving no reply as her sister stormed out of the room, slamming the door behind her. "I will get you some tea if you—Esther?"

Nothing but silence followed, and Lucy sat heavily back on her chair. *What on earth had got into her sister?* It was most unlike her to keep a letter from Arabella to herself, and to be so flushed at reading it—unless there was some great scandal in Bath, one they should all know about. It was most unaccountable.

Lucy looked around the dining room. The table was covered with festoons of brown paper, ribbons, string...but now that she was alone, a thrilling idea crossed her mind.

Why, if Esther did not need her here...

It took but eleven minutes for Lucy to creep out to the hall, pull on a pelisse—she was almost sure it was Sophia's, but the baby of the family would not mind—a pair of gloves and her bonnet, and quietly shut the front door behind her.

It was not as though she was precisely forbidden from leaving the house on her own; she was out in Society, and that meant it was perfectly acceptable to go visiting with her Mama or any one of her sisters, though Sophia could not formally be out until she or Esther married. *Lord, what a thought!*

But the direction of Lucy's steps was one her family would roll their eyes at, smile at, tease her that she had no business going and calling on gentleman.

Which was ridiculous. Lucy had never needed a reason to go calling on Percy. He was *Percy.*

The Ardingley residence was only a few streets across London from the Fitzroy home, and though the temperatures were freezing, Lucy warmed up quickly as she strode down the bustling streets, turning off into the quiet avenue with joy.

She was almost there—and then she would see him again. A warmth soared through her heart at the thought. Why, it had been almost two days since she had seen him. *A lifetime!*

Reaching the gate of the Ardingley home, she took a deep breath, and called out.

Phhooeee!

It did not take long. Within a minute, the front door opened and Viscount Percy Ardingley appeared, all joyous lopsided grin and tousled hair, one arm in a great coat and the other holding a top hat.

"What do you want?" he teased.

Lucy grinned. "I am bored," she said with a laugh, "so I thought I would come and make you bored, too. Interested in a walk?"

Percy laughed as he managed to put his hat on, then pull his other arm through his sleeve. "Charming! Am I your last resort then, that you come a-calling?"

"Don't be a dolt," said Lucy good naturedly. There was no one like Percy for attempting to wind her up into a temper—and no one for managing it, if he really wished to. There was something about Percy that roused her blood; she could not explain it.

But today was not a day to be irritable. Today the sun was almost managing to shine, and it was almost Christmas, and she had the whole world before her.

"And what did her ladyship consider for her entertainment this fine day?" asked Percy in an imperious voice not unlike that of Lady Romeril's as he stepped outside and pulled the door shut behind him.

Lucy giggled. "Goodness, fancy being a ladyship? I am not certain I would want such a thing, would you?"

Percy flushed for some reason, though she could not understand why. It was a perfectly natural thing to say—after all, her sister was a countess, and Caroline gave herself so many airs it was difficult to know what was expected of a lady and what her sister did just to be silly.

"I am a viscount," he pointed out, stepping down the path to the gate and pulling it open. "Anyone who m-marries me will be a lady."

Lucy took his arm without waiting for it to be offered and rolled her eyes. "Gosh, I forgot."

"You forgot?" teased Percy as they strode companionably down the street, arm in arm. "How long have you known me, you nincompoop!"

Their laughter mingled in the freezing air, and all the tension and distress Lucy had experienced hearing Esther talk so strangely about gentlemen—and kisses—melted away.

Why was the world always so right when she was with Percy? Why was it easy with him, easier than with her sisters? Why did everything slot into place so simply when he was by her side?

She could not explain it, but then she did not need to. She had Percy. Why explain a friendship that transcended words?

"Let's go down to the river," Lucy suggested as they turned onto the busier, bustling street. "We can watch the boats, see what kind are coming in this Christmas."

"I am amenable to that," said Percy. "While I remember, what—"

"It's so like the Christmas carol, isn't it?" said Lucy eagerly as they stepped around a gaggle of children staring at a toy ship on the river. "I saw three ships a sailing in—"

"You are always interrupting me, Miss Lucy Fitzroy, and I will not have it!"

Lucy grinned at Percy's mock outrage. "Me? Interrupting? What a slur onto my good nature, sir!"

Percy squeezed her hand in his arm, and Lucy returned it, joy twisting happily in her heart.

There was nothing else like this—walking along with Percy, their words intermingling as they interrupted each other, discussing the day, putting the world to rights, exploring London together, avoiding dry invitations to dull card parties, and promenades in the parks of the city.

No, she would take this, this moment, laughter, foolishness with Percy any day.

Why yearn for a husband, all that silly romance, the courting, the confusion, the misunderstandings and then the staid, uncomfortable proposal? Why wish for all that…when she had a best friend like Percy?

Chapter Two

LUCY TOOK A deep, calming breath. She was not going to lose her temper. *She wasn't.*

At least not here in the drawing room, right in front of her parents and Sophia. She would never live it down, she was sure, and she had spent what felt like all her life attempting to demonstrate that fiery red hair did not mean a fiery red temper.

Even if it did.

But really, she was being most provoked. What had Esther been thinking, purchasing a ticket to the opera for her—then insisting she accompanied her?

When had Lucy ever shown any interest in attending the opera?

Oh, that dull singing no one could understand, the music that went on and on—the formal gown one had to wear, all discomfort and stays—when the alternative was staying here, at home, roasting chestnuts over the fire and hearing her Papa tell stories of Christmases past?

It was little comfort that Esther had also invited two others.

"If you have invited two dull gentlemen—"

"That is no way to speak to your sister," came the sharp reproof of their father.

Lucy swallowed down the retort that was precisely how she wanted to speak to her sister, even if Esther did not deserve it, after she saw the look on her sister's face.

There was pain there—pain and confusion.

Lucy took another, slow breath. She did love her sister, all of them really. There was nothing like a Fitzroy to stand by another Fitzroy—or hurt another Fitzroy.

The wind whistled outside, the gloomy darkness hidden by the drawn curtains. Lucy shivered, despite the warmth from the blazing fire where Sophia sat. It was most unfair to force her from the home into the cold of the night—and all for an opera!

"I apologize," said Lucy stiffly. "But I have no wish to spend the evening with dullards who cannot string a sentence together and think the height of humor is—"

"I will be accompanied by the Duke of Kendal," Esther said quietly, in such a low voice it was almost impossible for Lucy to catch her words.

The Duke of Kendal!

A duke?

"But you hardly know him!" Lucy had not intended the words to fall from her mouth so easily, but really, she was most provoked!

Was this the end of their sisterly companionship? She stared at Esther, who was flushing most profusely. Was it possible that her sister...and the Duke of Kendal...

"And," said Esther hurriedly, "I invited Percy. He has accepted—he will be there soon, waiting for us."

Now that was different. Lucy's frown disappeared in a moment, her face softening at the sound of her friend's name. Percy? Attending the opera with them—oh, it was perfect. The two of them could jest at the others, all those primped and carefully attired fools who only came to the opera to be seen, to be admired, rather than enjoy the spectacle before them.

An evening with Percy!

Lucy grinned. "Well, why on earth did you not say so? Wait for me to change, won't you?"

She certainly could not attend the opera dressed like this, in a simple day gown of cotton with no adornments whatsoever.

Rushing out of the drawing room and up the stairs, Lucy burst into her bedchamber and started fumbling with the fastenings of her gown. Why, only yesterday Percy had joked with her at the docks that it would not be long before they would have to start attending more events in the Season or risk losing their Almack's vouchers—and was this not the perfect opportunity to do so?

Lucy's heart beat slightly painfully at the thought of her and Percy in the dark …which made no sense. It was Percy. There was no reason for her heart to be so excited.

She swiftly pulled on a silk gown—one almost past its best, she saw with a shake of her head, some of the stitching almost undone—and adorned herself with a string of pearls which had once belonged to Caroline.

Now she came to think about it, didn't they still belong to Caroline?

Lucy hesitated at the looking glass, trying to recall whether she had borrowed them, stolen them, or they had just mysteriously come into her possession. That was the thing with sisters. One never could tell.

Shrugging at her reflection and consoling herself with the thought that Caroline would never know anyway, Lucy hurtled downstairs and pulled on a pelisse, fur, and bonnet. They were almost certainly hers, at least. Probably.

When she pulled open the front door, heart thundering, it was to see with astonishment that the poor footman was shivering in the cold, the door to the carriage open—and Esther nowhere to be seen.

Lucy rolled her eyes as she slammed the front door. How typical of Esther; she was the one who wished to be off, was she not? Yet where was she?

Lucy hurtled back into the room. "What are you laughing at? Are you ready, Esther, we don't want to keep Percy waiting. Are we taking the carriage? Is that what you're wearing?"

Esther frowned at her, which made absolutely no sense.

"We're laughing at Papa, I am ready, we are taking the carriage, this is what I'm wearing," said Esther in a rush. "What's wrong with it?"

Lucy hesitated. Now that she came to think about it, she could not precisely explain it. There was something different about Esther, something she could not explain.

"I do not know, you just look…different," said Lucy, pulling on a pair of gloves.

"Good different?"

What on earth did it matter? They were only going to see Percy after all—and a duke, she supposed, but Lucy could not imagine that Esther had truly set her sights on him. He was a duke!

"Just different," shrugged Lucy. "Come on, we'll be late!"

She returned to the hall, stepping outside into the cold London air and breathed in deeply. Christmas was a time for treating herself, after all, and it would be a treat to spend time with Percy. Every moment with him was a gift.

Lucy waited at least ten minutes, or at least it felt that way, but eventually she stomped back into the drawing room to hear someone speaking.

"Are…well, are you sure that—"

"I thought you wanted to go to this opera!" Lucy said to Esther with a laugh. "Come on!"

Opening the drawing room door, Lucy saw with surprise their older sister Caroline had arrived, still brushing a little ice from her boots. *Thank goodness she had pulled the fur around her neck tight,* Lucy thought with a wicked grin. There was no possibility of her sister seeing the accidentally purloined necklace.

"Yes, Lucy, I am coming," said Esther, hastily stepping toward her. "Do not concern yourself Caroline, everything is under control, and we will certainly wrap up warm, Papa. Do not wait up, Mama, we will be late."

Under control? Lucy stared as Esther came into the hall and started to put an arm through her pelisse. *Under control? What was under control?*

The Duke of Kendal, eh? She knew better than to ask Esther precisely what was going on with such a gentleman—she would not get a straight answer, and besides, Lucy was determined to ask Percy's opinion of it all. He would have the chance to see the two of them together.

Something strange pulled in her stomach. A sensation of…warmth. Desire. Want.

It was gone as quickly as she had noticed it. Lucy swallowed, trying desperately to fathom what on earth that could have been. She had been thinking of Percy, of the opera…then that strange feeling. *What did it all mean?*

"If you do not hurry up, we shall be late," she said, more to distract herself than anything else.

"Yes, yes," murmured Esther distractedly.

"Come on!"

"Are we picking up Percy on the way?" asked Lucy as she clambered into the carriage. "Goodness, it's perishing in here!"

"No, we will meet both of them at the opera house," Esther replied as she, too, entered the carriage. "Drive on!"

One of the many benefits of living in London, Lucy had always thought, was that nothing was particularly far away. With a good carriage and clear roads, one could be almost anywhere in the city within twenty minutes—and indeed, it did not feel much longer before the carriage was slowing, the opera house visible through the window.

"Careful!"

Lucy paid no heed to her sister as she half stepped, half fell out of the carriage. It was all too strange, this Duke of Kendal nonsense—a desperate need for normality, for the calming presence of Percy, overwhelmed her as she looked around the busy street.

It appeared everyone and their mother had decided that tonight was the perfect time to attend the opera—and indeed, as Lucy's eyes scanned the crowd, she could see many of their vague acquaintance.

But no Percy.

Disappointment sank into her stomach like a lead weight, as she had never known before. Where was he? Where was Percy? Her dependence on him was great, yes, but she had not expected to need him quite so badly. What was the evening, if not a disappointment without him?

"Where are they?" Lucy said, eagerly looking around. "Did you suggest—"

Phhooeee!

Lucy's heart soared. There he was—there it was. Their call. The call they had perfected years ago, when children. A special call between them, an immediate way to find each other, to call each other out of their homes and out into the adventurous streets of London.

At the very beginning, all four of the younger Fitzroy sisters had called with Percy, and he had called them…the four calling birds, he had teased them, and from Lucy's memory, they had pushed him into the Thames for that remark.

But now it was only her. Her and Percy.

Both the Fitzroy sisters looked in the direction of the whistle, and Lucy grinned to see a beaming Percy leaning against the opera house wall.

"There he is!" Lucy said happily, pushing through the crowd toward him. "Hie there, Percy, did you ever think this morning we'd be attending the opera tonight!"

"Well, hello there!" said Percy with a laugh. "Goodness, don't you scrub up well?"

Lucy carefully punched Percy on the arm, and he pretended to fall over in agony, her giggles accompanying his pathetic groans.

He really was an ass, she thought warmly. Why, there was no one like him to be so…so dramatic. So foolish. He always knew how to make her laugh.

"Do you know anything about this evening?" asked Percy,

straightening up and raising an eyebrow. "I received a short note from Esther, of all people, saying my presence was required this evening."

Lucy rolled her eyes. "I am entirely in the dark, I assure you—there is something very odd going on, and I wish to know your opinion."

Interest flickered in Percy's face as he casually reached out, took her hand in his, and placed it in his arm. "My word, an intrigue?"

"Nothing so sordid, I can assure you!" said Lucy with a grin. "But it is too complicated to explain—just bear in mind that I wish to know your opinions on him when the evening is over."

Percy's face fell as they strode toward the opera house doors. "Him?"

But Lucy had no time to explain; Esther and the Duke of Kendal, a gentleman they had both been introduced to by Caroline but a fortnight ago, were waiting for them, both their faces flushed.

Which was strange. It was remarkably cold, even Lucy would admit it through her fur and pelisse. What on earth was going on?

But her interest in Esther's secrets faded as Lucy glanced upward at Percy's face. There was a gentleman to be proud of, a man she would never have to concern herself with. Discourtesy was not in Percy's nature, even if mischievousness was.

She looked over at the Duke of Kendal and grinned. "This is Percy."

As she knew she would, Esther blushed. It was a little wild, even Lucy would admit, introducing someone to a duke like that.

But it appeared that the Duke of Kendal did not mind. "Jack," he said, bowing. "I have heard much about you."

"Goodness, I haven't heard anything about you at all," said Percy with his typical laugh. "Have you known the family long?"

"About three weeks," said Jack cheerfully. "I was introduced by Cheshire."

"Cheshire?"

Lucy nudged Percy with her elbow and mouthed Walsingham as the four of them entered the opera house and started up toward the red velvet stairs.

"Oh, you mean Walsingham!" said Percy with a grin. "I forget sometimes he's managed to snag a fancy title, rather impressive though I say so myself. I am only a lord."

"And I am the Duke of Kendal," said Jack smoothly. "But who is counting?"

The two gentlemen laughed as they reached the box, and a shiver rushed through Lucy's spine. It was odd, suddenly not being a part of the conversation. She and Percy were usually the ones laughing together—laughing at the world, laughing—with affection, of course—at her sisters, laughing at the nonsense Society demanded of them during a Season.

And so, it was a moment before Lucy recognized the emotion curling around her heart as they reached the landing and started walking toward the boxes.

Jealousy.

She was jealous—jealous of Percy. It was a remarkably strange thought, but Lucy could not deny it. Sharing Percy was not something she did often, and now to see him chattering away to another…it was odd.

Most unpleasant.

They reached the box Esther had chosen before Lucy could untangle all her thoughts, and they stood there waiting for her sister, as the benefactress of that evening, to enter first. But she was simply standing there, saying nothing, eyes glazed over.

Lucy cleared her throat. Well, there was little else she could do to aid her sister, and she was behaving most oddly. What was she supposed to do?

Glancing up at Percy, she saw him shrug and raise his eyebrows. So, he had noticed it too; of course, he had. There was no one like Percy for noticing things.

And once again that strange hot molten sensation pooled into her stomach. What was it? What on earth did it mean?

"Are you ready to go in?" asked the Duke of Kendal to her sister. "I had not realized you had purchased an entire box."

"Yes—yes, of course," Esther said with a nervous smile, which made no sense to Lucy. "In we go."

Stepping forward, she opened the door and welcomed them in. Lucy swiftly saw that six seats had been placed in the box, all elegantly positioned to afford each occupant a perfect view of the stage.

"Here, Percy, let's take these two," she said, seating herself at the very right end of the row.

Percy obliged by sitting beside her, and Lucy watched as Esther and the Duke of Kendal took the two seats on the other end, leaving two seats between them.

Now why on earth had Esther not mentioned she had purchased a box? Her parents could have attended, and Selina Fitzroy adored the opera. It was most unaccountable—unless she had not known that six seats would be provided?

"How on earth did you afford this?" came the quiet question from the Duke of Kendal at the other end of the row.

"Easily, I am afraid."

Lucy rolled her eyes. Esther had never been very good at hiding their wealth, especially her dowry. Why did she think so many gentlemen kept asking their Papa for her hand?

"How long until the wedding?"

Lucy gasped at the indecorous question asked by the Duke of Kendal—and saw the flush on her sister's face.

Well. So, there it was; that accounted for everything. The Duke of Kendal was in love with her sister—and from the splutters and muttered conversation she could now no longer catch, it appeared Esther was in love with the Duke of Kendal.

Goodness—a duchess in the family! Lucy had considered it rather wild that Caroline was a countess, but this was even more ridiculous.

At least that explained why Esther had wished for her and Percy to attend with her—and why their parents had not been considered. Lucy grinned at the idea of sitting with a gentleman one was in love with their parents seated beside them. *How awful!*

"Penny for your thoughts?"

Lucy turned to grin at Percy. "It doesn't matter, I have worked it all out now."

There was a quizzical expression on his face. "Worked it all—"

"You do not have to worry yourself about it, I assure you," Lucy said cheerfully. *Well, well, another Fitzroy marriage!* "Though I suppose we shall have to suffer through—"

Her words were interrupted by the sudden beginning of the music, the orchestra crashing into a minor chord, preventing Percy from hearing her.

Not that it mattered. There would be plenty of opportunities, Lucy knew, to speak with Percy about it all. She would greatly appreciate his opinion, particularly on the duke himself—who knew what a man like that was really like?

As the performers stepped onto the stage, the curtain rustling back, Lucy settled herself in her seat. Well, if they were here, she may as well enjoy herself.

"Lucy—"

"Shh," she said without looking at Percy.

"But I...I wanted to talk to you about—"

The singing began, and despite all of Lucy's bad temper when she had first been informed of the outing, she was transported. There was nothing like music, music like this, music that surely angels would—

"Lucy, I must tell you something," came the urgent, hurried whisper of Percy beside her.

Lucy dragged her eyes from the stage and glared at Percy, her expression softening immediately as it always did when she looked at him. It was impossible to be irritated with this man for more than five minutes, more's the pity. How many times has she attempted it?

"What?" she murmured.

Percy opened his mouth, but no words came out. It was most

unaccountable; they had never been worried about speaking to each other, nothing had been borne between them, no topic so difficult it could not be discussed.

Slightly distracted by the whispers at the other end of the short row, Lucy turned to stare at her sister, who appeared most uncomfortable, then back to Percy.

"Do you think…do you think they love each other?"

For some unknown reason, Percy's cheeks tinged. At least, that was what it looked like in the darkness of the opera house. Lucy could have been mistaken—she must be. It made no sense for Percy to be embarrassed about Esther's wild behavior.

Movement, just out of the corner of her eye. Lucy watched agog, mouth open, as her sister and the Duke of Kendal rose without a word and left the box. The door shut behind them with a snap.

"Well!" breathed Lucy, turning to Percy with wide eyes. "Where are they going?"

But Percy did not appear to care about Esther or the Duke of Kendal or whatever they could be getting up to. He was looking at her, his attention entirely fixed upon her.

Lucy closed her mouth. It was strange, this look of his. She had never seen Percy look so…so…

Well. Intense. There was no other word for it. His normally lively eyes were sharp, focused, as though he had been bid to memorize her face. There was such intensity in his face that Lucy, despite herself, found heat searing her cheeks.

She was…blushing. Blushing in front of Percy! What on earth was going on today?

"I wanted to tell you something," said Percy in a low, urgent voice.

Lucy swallowed. Her stomach was fluttering most outlandishly, and all she could think of was that it was in response to Percy's oddness today.

Speak to her? He spoke to her all the time. Tell her something? What could it possibly be that he had to be this bizarre about it?

Lucy gasped—she could not help it, the searing contact between her hand and Percy's had utterly astonished her. His fingers, always so strong, always so certain, were hesitant. Warm. Questing, moving between hers to entwine them.

Heart racing, lungs tight, and absolutely none the wiser as to why her body was reacting in such an odd way to Percy, of all people, Lucy looked into Percy's eyes.

The questions that rose from her heart died away on her lips. This was Percy, her best friend. At times, she rather thought she was closer to him than any of her sisters, not that she would ever admit to as much in the Fitzroy household.

Of course, if he wanted to tell her something, she would listen.

"Percy?" Lucy breathed.

Percy nodded, his eyes inexplicably drifting to her lips for a moment before returning to her eyes.

Lucy swallowed. Her stomach really was misbehaving; perhaps it was something odd she ate before she came out to the opera this evening.

"Lucy," said Percy quietly, not looking away from her. "I…well, I have wanted to tell you for some time, and there has never been a good moment."

Though she wished to speak, Lucy found she could not. Her hands were scalding, searing heat flowing from his to hers, and she did not understand it. This was Percy. Why was he having such an effect on her? It was Percy.

"We are…we are the best of friends," said Percy hesitantly.

Lucy nodded. That was not up for discussion.

"And I was thinking—though this may surprise you—that perhaps we—"

"Oh, look!"

Lucy had not intended to interrupt him, she really hadn't, but it was impossible not to. Fireworks had sparked on the stage, sparks flying in all directions as the singers were illuminated by their flames, and the entire opera house gasped and applauded at the spectacle.

Dragging her hand away from Percy, Lucy clapped along with them, looking over at her companion with a wide grin. "Can you believe they attempted such a thing?"

For some reason, Percy looked remarkably unimpressed. *Well, there is no accounting for taste*, Lucy thought as her heart thumped painfully in her chest. A reaction to the fireworks, of course.

What else could it be?

CHAPTER THREE

"—AND THEN THE way she died at the end—so spectacular! Almost throwing herself off the stage, absolutely impossible to believe she wasn't hurt." Lucy gushed, freezing hands clasped before her as they walked slowly along the street. "Don't you think?"

She would not have normally asked the question; she would not have had to.

After the opera ended, full of enormous efforts from the performers and far more fireworks than Lucy thought strictly necessary, they had emerged from the opera house to find a light dusting of snow. It was still drifting gently down, and Lucy, ever the romantic, had sent back the carriage.

"After all, who would not want a walk home in the snow?" she had said at the time to the strangely quiet Percy. "When was the last time you can remember it snowing this close to Christmas?"

Percy had not replied. He had not said anything, now Lucy came to think of it, since they had left the opera house. They had been walking for a little time now, perhaps ten minutes, but still he remained silent, no matter how much Lucy talked. *Most strange.*

Lucy glanced sideways at the gentleman beside her, matching her pace, leaving boot prints in the snow. Percy's tousled hair under his top hat was just as it always was—dark and untamed, curling in some areas and sticking out at others. His eyes were strangely serious, his chiseled jaw taut.

There was evidently something on his mind. Something worrying him, consuming him, preventing him from hearing her delightful commentary on the opera itself.

Lucy's stomach twisted. Seeing Percy like this...it was unpleasant in a way she had never experienced. Percy was never silent. Quiet, yes. Shy sometimes with other people. It was rare, but she had seen it.

But with her? There was never anything they hid from each other, nothing too difficult to say that forced them into such solitude. *What was going on?*

Percy caught her eye and attempted to smile.

Attempted was the right word for it, Lucy thought desperately. There was no real joy in those eyes, no genuine happiness. A forced smile, for her!

Things must be very bad indeed.

"Lucy. I...well, I have wanted to tell you for some time, and there has never been a good moment."

Lucy bit her lip. He had attempted to tell her something during the opera, and for all her complaints about going in the first place, she had been transported by the performance. So transported she had neglected to see what was right in front of her.

Her best friend needed her.

The snow started to fall more heavily, settling on their shoulders as Lucy and Percy turned a corner onto a broader street, an avenue of saplings planted on each side. The snow had already settled on their branches, giving them an elegant yet eerie appearance.

"I...I enjoyed the opera," said Lucy. "Did you?"

Percy sighed but said nothing.

Lucy swallowed. Perhaps there was something wrong beyond her initial estimation. Could his mother, still in the country, be unwell? He had no siblings to speak of—a sister twelve years older, who he hardly knew, hardly counted—but perhaps there was trouble there?

"I considered jumping onto the opera stage myself and revealing my undergarments," Lucy said conversationally, keeping a close eye on Percy's reactions. "Do you think that would have been a good idea?"

"What?" said Percy distractedly, as though she had interrupted him from a deep sleep.

Lucy stared.

His gaze had sparked toward her but swiftly drifted away to the pavement before them. Lucy tightened her fingers together, wishing she had not left her gloves in the opera house. What on earth was wrong with him?

Could it be something she said?

"And I was thinking—though this may surprise you—that perhaps we—"

"Oh, look!"

Lucy took a deep breath. Whatever it was weighing on Percy's heart, it would undoubtedly injure her just as it was hurting him; but that was what friends were for, was it not? And they were not merely friends, they were…best friends.

Something odd stirred within Lucy, a fiery intensity, a determination to see him happy, to prevent any harm from ever coming from him.

It was not territorial, exactly—she was not entirely sure she could describe it, for the emotion was not one she had ever felt before.

Whatever it was, it consumed her, burning through all her fear, consuming the panic she had felt, and leaving nothing but resolve. A desperate desire to ensure he was happy and heard and safe.

Lucy unclasped her hands and slipped one into the hand hanging beside him. "Percy."

There was no reply. Percy's gaze was still drifting away as

though focused on something entirely different.

It was not a conscious thought, more an unconscious action. Swallowing momentarily, Lucy pursed her lips together.

Phhooeee!

Percy jerked, his whole body responding, and his gaze focused on the here and now. He turned, a slow smile creeping across his face, and the painful knot which had been tightening in Lucy's stomach started to unravel.

"There you are," she said softly.

"I was miles away," said Percy ruefully. "Have I—goodness, how did we get here?"

He looked around, eyes wide with astonishment, at the avenue they were walking along, as though Lucy had somehow managed to transport him by magic.

"We…we walked," Lucy replied, a little astonished at his lack of attention, but unwilling to critique him for such daydreaming. Not before she knew precisely what it was crowding his mind. "What is wrong with you this evening?"

But Percy did not reply. He continued to walk, the hasty pace of his gait unceasing, and Lucy had no choice but to walk alongside him.

Still, this was one of her favorite things to do, walk alongside Percy. There was a strength, a certainty in Percy's strides she had seen in no other.

Percy's fingers tightened around hers, and a flare of heat, unbidden and uncontrolled, seared through Lucy's body. A match set aflame to her limbs, every inch of her tingling inexplicably, the cold of the snow and the wintery wind nothing to the blaze within her.

Lucy almost staggered, her feet heavy, her mind unable to comprehend what was happening.

Where did this fire come from, this warmth, this—this yearning?

"Lucy?"

Percy's hand, strong and stable, prevented Lucy from collapsing to her feet, holding her upright as his concerned eyes met hers.

"I-I am quite well," Lucy stammered.

She had never felt less well in her life—yet the sensations were not unpleasant. To the contrary, now they had stopped her head spinning, they had a rather warm and pleasant tinge to them, though the intensity of the heat was dying away.

What had started such forceful sensations? Where had they come from, and now they were dissipating…how could she feel them again?

"Holding your hand seems to be the only way to keep you on your feet," said Percy with a chuckle.

Lucy attempted to smile. She could never tell Percy what she had just experienced, of course; it would be scandalous, even she could see that, to admit to such…such desires.

Desires she did not understand.

Percy would not understand; he would laugh, or worse, revile her for such things. She could not explain them to herself, let alone attempt to describe them to Percy.

She shivered unconsciously at the very thought of revealing such outrageous tendencies. No, it was best Percy did not know. He would not understand, would not wish to.

"Do you remember when we first did that?"

Lucy looked at Percy, unsure precisely what he meant. When they first walked alone together? Far too long ago. When they had first gone to the opera together? Goodness, the number of times she had been forced to trot out to the opera during her first Season…it was a miracle she had Percy there to distract her from the utter unbelievable looks she and all the other new debutantes were receiving.

Percy appeared to understand her confusion. "When we first held hands."

He lifted their clasped hands. Lucy smiled at the sight of her fingers intertwined with Percy's. With anyone else, it would be an intimate act, one suggesting far more romantic tendencies than they had ever shared with each other.

But with Percy…well. It felt right. He had never asked to take her hand, and she had never asked to take his. They did not need to.

True, they rarely did such a thing in public—the last thing she needed was for some gossip to spread the rumor that they were engaged to be married. *The very thought!*

A smile crept across Lucy's face, disappearing swiftly as the realization that one day, Percy Ardingley would be engaged to another swept through her mind.

Percy, someone else's. Percy, the husband of another woman—Percy, no longer able to hold her hand like this as they meandered home, because it would be most outrageous to consider such a thing.

Percy, not hers.

Lucy shivered, though the movement had little to do with the cold. No, she would not even think on such a thing. It was outrageous to think it.

Percy was…well, Percy. Lucy had no brothers, but what she felt for him was surely what one felt for any male sibling.

Was it not?

"Lucy?"

Lucy started and found it was she this time who had not been conscious of their walking, seeing they had now reached the furthest end of her street. At the other end was her home, and the end of her walk with Percy.

She slowed her pace, and Percy immediately adjusted to match her.

She smiled. That was the wonderful thing about Percy—one of the wonderful things, rather. He did not always need explanations. Most of the time he simply knew what she was thinking, and agreed.

It was like having someone else able to read one's thoughts.

"I cannot remember the first time we held hands," Lucy admitted, a wry smile on her face. "We have known each other so long, it is hard to untangle some memories."

Percy chuckled. "Like the time you decided to get on a boat to Africa, running away from home?"

"That was a misunderstanding," contradicted Lucy with a grin. "I merely wished to visit. I had no intention of actually staying! Besides, what about the time I had to rescue you from purchasing that pig at Southwark Market!"

"I was hungry!" protested Percy, laughing. "I do not think it would have been so difficult to walk back home."

The two of them laughed, multitudes of memories soaring through the air between them, so real Lucy could almost see them. So many adventures, so many times they had shared. Tears when frustrated, embraces when celebrating. If she did not have Esther or one of her sisters beside her, it was Percy.

It was always Percy.

"Well, here we are."

Lucy blinked. Here they were indeed—right outside her parents' home. There was still a light on in the hallway, doubtless left by Mrs. Castle, the housekeeper, to ensure Lucy did not crash about the place when she came in.

It had only been the one time; she did not know why Mama kept going on about it.

"Here we are," she repeated.

Her hand was still closely encircled by Percy's, yet she made no movement to go inside. Now she was here, it was rather like a little bereavement, to go inside and let go of Percy. Let go of the connection.

"Lucy," said Percy quietly.

Lucy stepped around to face Percy, her hand still in his. "Yes?"

His eyes were serious, eyelashes tinged with snow. Lucy could not help but smile as she looked into his face. Who could help it? He was a handsome man, Percy—at least, she supposed he was. He was just Percy to her, but she had to admit that those features on anyone else would be handsome indeed.

That strange warmth flickered in her stomach—slightly be-low her stomach. It was most unaccountable.

"Lucy, this Christmas I…I wanted to get you something special."

Lucy nodded. It did not appear Percy needed a response to that, but at the same time, he seemed unable to continue.

What was he trying to say?

"And…and the more I thought about it, the more difficult it became to think of something to get you," Percy continued, his voice low, earnest, his eyes raking over her face. "I thought…I thought maybe we were planning to…to get each other the same Christmas gift."

Lucy swallowed. Somehow this lighthearted conversation had become…well. Serious.

There was a serious look in Percy's eyes, one she had never seen before, and that warmth gathered pace, flickering into flames and soaring through her body. For some reason, her breathing was a little difficult.

The way he looked at her like that…it was unlike any look Percy had ever given her.

Lucy's heart skipped a beat as Percy took her other hand in his.

They had never stood like this before, mere inches apart, hand in hand, as though…as though he was about to confess something to her. As though he had something to tell her that was of such great import.

"The…same thing?" Lucy whispered.

She did not know why she whispered. She had intended to speak clearly, rationally, like a person would in a normal conversation.

Was that her pulse she could feel, or Percy's?

"I have wanted to tell you," said Percy in a low voice, "for…well. A long time."

Lucy looked at him, still unsure precisely what he meant.

For though she could not explain it, and though it was remarkably not an unpleasant feeling but rather an unexpected one, she was finding herself…well. Drawn to Percy.

Not in the normal way. She was always drawn to Percy; he was one of her favorite people in the whole world. But in this moment, inexplicable as it was, she was…drawn to him. Physically. As though she wished to close the gap between them.

Lucy's gaze drifted from his eyes to his lips. Suddenly, she was highly conscious of them. They were rather pleasant to look at. What would they be like to touch—to kiss?

Heat seared her cheeks as the thought occurred to her, but to Lucy's astonishment, it did not dissipate the thought—if anything, it merely increased it. What would it be like to kiss Percy, to feel his lips on hers, to know the warmth of his passion, passion he would certainly never have for her.

And she had none for him, Lucy reminded herself as that strange warmth pooled between her legs once more. Not at all. Not in the slightest. It was Percy, for goodness's sake. The idea of kissing him ought to be repellant, and why it was so pleasing, and warming, she could not understand.

Percy shifted slightly. He was closer, somehow, and was his gaze now on her lips? Perhaps Lucy was seeing things—but now she was leaning, tilting her head, and she could not explain nor would she stop it, for he was drifting closer, his lips tantalizingly—

"Lucy! Thank goodness, there you are!"

The front door to the Fitzroy home had opened, and in that instant, Lucy and Percy sprang apart. There in the doorway stood her mother, hair up in rags and face creased with concern.

"Mama!" Lucy did not know whether it was instinct or shame or something else that had forced her away from Percy in that moment, but she greatly regretted the cessation of contact.

Having him beside her, before her, close to her…that had felt wonderful. Wonderful in a new way—a way she was not sure she wanted to understand.

"My dear Mrs. Fitzroy, what is it?" said Percy urgently.

Lucy glanced at him, then back at her mother, and saw all the signs of something truly terrible. She had never seen her mother like this. Her eyes were wide, searching behind them as though waiting for someone, her fingers were white as they clutched at the doorframe.

"Esther," said Selina Fitzroy urgently. "She is not with you?"

"Of course not," said Lucy dismissively. "Why, despite all her demands that I attend the opera with her, she and the Duke of Kendal left before the first act was finished. She would have got here hours ago."

Percy stepped forward to place a comforting hand on her mother's arm, and Lucy loved him for it. It was a special sort of friend who cared so much for one's mother, after all.

"But that is just it—Esther is not here!" her Mama said wildly. "She never came home. She never made it back from the opera!"

Lucy's mouth fell open. "Not—not here?"

"I am sure there is a perfectly reasonable explanation," said Percy soothingly, placing his other hand on Lucy's arm, but she shrugged him off.

Strange sensations, odd longings, and a most puzzling desire to kiss Percy notwithstanding, she had something far more important to worry about.

"Esther is missing?" she said, stepping forward as her mother moved to permit her inside the house. "*Missing?*"

"Missing with the Duke of Kendal," Percy repeated quietly.

Esther would never...

"But if a gentleman kissed you, Lucy...what would you do?"

Lucy's face fell. "No, she would not...they would not have...eloped?"

Her mother shot her a warning look, then glanced at Percy for good measure.

It took Lucy a moment to understand quite what her mother was suggesting, then she rolled her eyes. Percy Ardingley? They could speak freely before him; he was not likely to take that tidbit to the gossip mill. It would not be Percy's fault if this scandal got into the newspapers.

Percy cleared his throat. "I imagine you will wish for privacy as you consider…as you find Esther. Good evening, Mrs. Fitzroy. Lucy, think about…about what I said."

Lucy blinked. What he said? She could barely recall what Percy had said—not now her sister might have eloped with a duke…

CHAPTER FOUR

LUCY HAD NEVER known such tension in the Fitzroy household. The entire building ached with it, pouring from every room, every crevice, every face.

She swallowed in the silence of the breakfast room. There they were, most of them.

Jemima would be arriving any time for Christmas, along with her husband Captain Hugh Rotherham; Caroline and Stuart had their own London townhouse but would be over later that afternoon; and Arabella was still in Bath. They had had not written to her, had not seen the point.

It had only been one night, after all. Esther and the Duke of Kendal could not have gone far.

Lucy awkwardly picked up a slice of toast and bit into it, hating the loud crunching noise that echoed. Sophia glanced at her, eyes red, and then at their mother, whose face was pale.

Putting the toast down, Lucy attempted to chew and swallow as quietly as possible. None of the Fitzroys had spoken since each of them descended for breakfast.

What was there to say? Though Lucy and her Mama had stayed up until four o'clock in the morning, there was no sign, no word from Esther. They had finally slipped into sleep on the sofa in the drawing room, but when Mrs. Castle awoke them—to their mutual astonishment—at six o'clock, there was still no

Esther.

No Esther. Lucy swallowed her toast, which scratched her throat, and tried not to think the worst. Esther could not be hurt, after all. She had left the opera quite willingly with the Duke of Kendal. He was not a man to hurt her.

Was he?

Lucy glanced at the door, as though it would magically open and reveal her sister, alive and well.

It was a strange thing indeed, when one hoped their sister had eloped and married a duke. Better that than the alternative, that they were not married…or worse still, that something awful had befallen her. Perhaps befallen both of them.

"Has…has anyone gone to the Duke of Kendal's residence?" Lucy spoke the words hesitantly, knowing it would be painful for his name to be spoken.

Her Papa nodded. "I went there last night after you returned, and first thing this morning. The servant there said his master had not come home."

Lucy nodded silently. Well, whatever had happened to Esther had likely happened to the Duke of Kendal, too, though that was little comfort.

A sudden sob broke the silence, and the everyone looked at Selina Fitzroy.

"What if they were hurt on the way to be married?" she cried, tears overspilling onto her cheeks. "What if they were robbed, attacked, murdered!"

"I am sure nothing of the sort has happened," said Arthur Fitzroy hastily.

"Surely not," said Sophia, her face not entirely marrying up with her words.

Lucy shook her head. Her throat was suddenly dry, and she could not speak. What if, what if…no one could possibly win this "what if" game. They did not know what had happened to Esther, they did not know where she was, who she was with,…and they seemed no closer to knowing now than when they had first realized she had not come home.

If only Percy was here.

The thought fluttered through her mind before she could examine it. Not that she needed to. It was natural to wish for her best friend to be here, the friend who could perhaps console her, give ideas as to where Esther might be. Safe and well.

And married, ideally, Lucy thought wryly, though wild horses would not have dragged that particular thought from her. As her sister and father tried to comfort her mother, Lucy tried desperately not to think what would happen if Esther was unharmed but also unmarried.

It would certainly be a death knell for Sophia's marriage prospects, she thought darkly. And hers, too, she supposed. She rarely thought about it, and it seemed odd to be so concerned about that when Esther was missing.

"—not concern myself?" her mother was saying wretchedly to something her husband had just said. "Our daughter is missing!"

The words echoed around the breakfast room, and a lead weight fell into Lucy's stomach. Missing. Esther. It did not seem real—not possible. Where on earth was she?

The door to the hall opened, and all four of them turned instantly to it.

"Happy Christmas Eve!" trilled Caroline as she entered, all beaming smiles and flakes of snow. "Goodness, still at breakfast, I wondered why you were not in the…in the…"

Her voice faded away as her gaze took in the sight of them: her mother crying, Sophia's eyes red rimmed, and serious looks on both her father and Lucy's face.

"What on earth has happened?" Caroline said quietly. "Is it Jemima—Esther? Arabella? Are they—"

"I told him we would be here before luncheon, and here we are!"

Lucy almost laughed at the ridiculousness of it. Just when they needed a little quiet and calm, it appeared every Fitzroy in the world was about to appear.

Behind Caroline was Jemima, still dressed in a traveling cloak, a triumphant smile on her face as her husband, Captain Rotherham, appeared behind her, smiling wryly.

"I did not say that we would not be here before luncheon," he said, in the tone of someone reminding another of the true facts of a conversation. "In that, what I actually said was...my dear Selina, what is it?"

Too late, Lucy realized she should have attempted to take her two eldest sisters out of the breakfast room to explain the situation to them quietly—but as it was, she was too late.

Her mother burst into devastated tears, words somewhere under her cries but entirely unintelligible. Her father rose hastily to put his arms around his wife.

"Mama!" Jemima's face had fallen, and though Lucy noticed her half-sister had called her stepmother by such an affectionate term—most unusually—she had no opportunity to remark on it. "What in goodness's name has happened?"

Both she and Caroline rushed toward Selina, the focus of the entire room on the sobbing matriarch.

Captain Rotherham turned to the rest of the table for answers, but before he could utter a word, Sophia started to sob, too.

Lucy sighed heavily. Well, it would all have to come out at some point. "Good morning, Hugh. The trouble is slight, we hope, though I think it is the unknown factors distressing Mama so. Esther—"

"Esther!" Selina cried.

Everyone turned to the doorway. There, a little disheveled, hair flowing down her shoulders, hem three inches damp, and an awkward smile on her face, stood Esther Fitzroy.

It was difficult to tell precisely who rushed to embrace her first. Lucy had certainly paid no heed to her chair as it tipped over, a rush of affectionate relief overpowering her, but Sophia managed to reach Esther before her, the both of them embracing their missing sister so hard it seemed to knock the breath out of her.

"Ah," said a voice Lucy did not recognize. "I see we have inadvertently concerned everyone."

Lucy released Esther, only for a moment, to look at the speaker—a similarly disheveled Duke of Kendal.

"You," she said threateningly, pointing a finger dramatically at the man, who was the cause of this nightmare. "You!"

"Your Grace," said her Papa stiffly as he straightened up. "I believe I have a few questions for—"

"I am afraid all that will have to wait, Papa," said Esther, managing to disentangle herself from Sophia, still sobbing just as violently as their mother. "I believe Jack will wish to talk to you about a great number of things, but that will have to wait. Everyone—we are engaged!"

Caroline squeaked, Jemima stared, and Lucy grabbed hold of Esther's shoulders and shook her.

"Engaged?" Lucy repeated, staring into her sister's eyes, her heart thumping wildly as the word started to sink in. "What—engaged to be married?"

It could not be true—though it would explain a few things. That nonsensical opera visit, for a start, and just why a joyous smile had crept across Esther's face.

"But if a gentleman kissed you, Lucy...what would you do?"

"I find myself utterly unable to live without your daughter, and so have asked her to marry me," said the Duke of Kendal blithely, as though this was something one announced all the time. "My word, I do hope we have not frightened any of you."

Understanding started to dawn in Lucy's mind as even more chaos erupted around her. Sophia was no longer sobbing, though their mother's tears had, if anything, only increased in volume and consistency.

Her Papa had stridden around the room and grabbed the Duke of Kendal's hand, most roughly in Lucy's opinion, Jemima was whispering hurriedly to her husband, and Mrs. Castle had rushed in following all the noise.

"It is true?" Lucy said quietly to Esther, who seemed unable to cease smiling. "You are engaged—you love him, Esther?"

"More than anything," said Esther happily. "More than I thought possible. More than riches, more than money, more than Christmas—where are you going?"

The question was not posited to Lucy, but rather to her betrothed to be, who was being pulled inexorably out of the room.

"Your duke and I have business to discuss," said their Papa firmly. "Come on, Your Grace."

The Duke of Kendal looked nervously at her sister, and Esther grinned back, a comforting, wordless look Lucy had never seen before.

Lucy swallowed, her breath slightly tight in her lungs. What was it to have someone like that in one's life, to know precisely what they were thinking with just a look? To share insight like that, across a crowded and noisy room, without words?

She could hardly imagine such a thing.

Well, she had Percy, of course, but it was not the same thing. She rarely had to explain anything to him, he understood her so well. Sometimes, better than she understood herself.

"Is anyone going to tell me what is going on?" asked Jemima sternly. "Sophia, pull yourself together, you're going to have a duchess as a sister! You'll be out for the next Season!"

"A daughter, a duchess!" murmured Selina rapturously.

"You already have a daughter who is a countess," pointed out Caroline, sitting in her father's seat and picking up his fork to nibble his bacon.

Sophia laughed through her tears, wiping them away with the back of her hand. "Goodness, do not raise the bar too much, I am not sure how many princes are still available!"

It was laughter now and not tears that filled the breakfast room as excited chatter rushed between them. Somehow, Lucy felt a little apart from it. As though it was happening just past her, through a glass window. Something she could see, but could not take part in.

She should feel happy for her sister, she knew that, but this was not happiness she felt. At least, not quite. There was some happiness there, some joy for Esther, but at the same time there was a morose sort of longing.

Esther would be married. She would be leaving the Fitzroy house as Jemima and Caroline had done before her. There would only be two of them now, herself and Sophia.

It was strange. The family was always so large, so noisy, filling up the place, but it was Esther who was the sister she was closest to. The one she relied on the most. And now she was leaving.

A nudge from an elbow brought her back to the present. "What?"

Esther grinned. "Can you believe it?"

"I cannot," said Lucy honestly with a laugh. "Goodness, you kept that quiet!"

"It all happened so quickly, I did not feel as though I had enough time to draw breath, let alone attempt to explain it to anyone," admitted Esther. "Though I attempted it once, with you. Do you not remember?"

Lucy nudged her sister back as she laughed. "All that nonsense about kissing—you dark horse, Esther, I had no idea!"

"You are a dullard indeed, then, I thought myself far too obvious," said Esther. "What on earth did you think I was talking about?"

It was a good question, but one Lucy did not have the time to answer.

"Esther Fitzroy, come here and give your mother a hug!"

Laughing, tears sparkling in Esther's eyes, she stepped forward to embrace their Mama.

Lucy quietly slipped out of the room. They did not seem to need her anymore anyway, and it meant she could go to the one person whose opinion she needed.

Phhooeee!

Hearing her call, Percy opened the door with a smile that appeared far more nervous than Lucy would have expected.

"Esther is engaged to be married," Lucy declared by way of greeting as she pushed her way past Percy into his house.

Something lurched in her stomach as she brushed up against him, something rather akin to the feelings she had experienced last night—but it was over almost before it had begun, and Lucy had stepped through into his drawing room without an invitation.

Well, she had never needed an invitation before, had she?

The comforting and calming presence of Percy and the familiarity of his drawing room had an immediate effect on Lucy as she sat down on the egg-blue embroidered sofa.

Ardingley House. How many times had she been here—a hundred? A thousand? She almost knew the place as well as her own home, she visited so frequently. Every inch of the room was known to her, from the delicately needle-worked screens by the fire to the gold clock over the mantelpiece.

"Engaged to be married?" repeated Percy as he followed her into the room and closed the door behind him. "Not missing, then?"

"Really, she was only missing twelve hours," said Lucy.

If they had just gone to bed when she had got home, they would only have realized Esther was absent for an hour, perhaps two. It would all have been quite a different affair.

"Engaged to whom?"

Lucy rolled her eyes. "Come on, Percy, think!"

Her teasing raised a smile as he stepped toward her. "Well then, I would guess—"

"It's the duke of course, the Duke of Kendal," Lucy said, cutting across him.

Percy folded his arms and raised an eyebrow. "That wasn't much of a chance to guess, was it?"

Lucy smiled. All the tension in her chest at the conflicting emotions she had felt upon hearing the news of Esther's engagement to the Duke of Kendal was starting to dissipate.

Happiness, guilt, confusion, sadness…they all started to fade away whenever she was with Percy, leaving only the happiness.

"Well, I am pleased for her," said Percy cheerfully, throwing himself into an armchair opposite her. "That is a remarkably good match for her, too, though if anyone deserved to marry a duke, it is Esther."

"Not me?"

"Not in the slightest," said Percy with a laugh, not rising to Lucy's bait. "You wouldn't want to dress up in that awfully formal stuff and go to court every other day, would you?"

Lucy scrunched up her nose. "Certainly not."

But now Esther would. It was a rather jolting thought, Esther moving into quite a different life. Yes, they would still be sisters, but it would not be the same.

Something of her thoughts must have showed on her face, for Percy cleared his throat. "You are jealous."

"Jealous?" Lucy focused on the man making such ridiculous statements. "What, me?"

"You," said Percy with a nod.

Was that a knowing smile on his face? How dare he look at her with a knowing smile! He had no idea what she was feeling—neither did she, if it came to that.

But now Lucy thought about it, a small part of her wondered…well. Whether he was right. This odd feeling, this emotion she had not understood nor been able to name…was it possible that it was jealousy?

Lucy had never desired a particularly impressive match for herself. In truth, she had given little thought to the match she would end up with. The idea of being a duchess had never appealed, but still…there was something in the way Esther had looked at the Duke of Kendal and been looked at in return.

Some sort of intimacy that they shared, far beyond what Lucy had ever experienced. Esther was experiencing something new, something Lucy could not accompany her for.

Was that where the jealousy came from?

"There, y'see," said Percy as though he'd presented an impressive argument. "You are jealous."

"Am not," retorted Lucy automatically.

He laughed as he rose to his feet, moving across the room to sit beside her. "I do not know why you attempt to deny it!"

"Because it is not true," Lucy insisted as she turned to face him, her hands beside her and now mere inches from his own.

It wasn't true…was it?

"You and Esther have spent so much time together, and now you will have to wave her goodbye as she enters a new stage of life," said Percy gently, all the mocking gone from his voice. "And you are still waiting for a gentleman to call your name and sweep you off your feet."

Lucy flushed, hating the heat warming her cheeks. It was not true—at least, she did not wish it to be true.

Was she waiting for a gentleman to sweep her off her feet? Lucy was not entirely sure what being swept off her feet would look like. No gentleman had ever tried to woo her—at least, not that she had recognized.

"What do I need a husband for," Lucy found herself saying, "when I have you?"

She saw in an instant that she had said something wrong.

Percy's eyes widened, his mouth fell open, and a most unusual flush tinged his cheeks. "Wh-What?"

Lucy swallowed. She was not entirely sure what she had meant. She was suddenly conscious of how close Percy was on the sofa—which was ridiculous. They were always close.

But not like this. Not so close that she could reach out and touch him, the instinct to do so somehow growing in her heart.

What would that achieve, she asked herself firmly.

It did not appear to matter that she had no answer. Just being close to him, being near him, was all she wanted. All she needed.

"We…we are best friends," Lucy managed to say, her mouth finally obeying her commands. "What else could I mean?"

She met his gaze, her whole body quivering. The intensity of his expression was…pleasurable.

Lucy could think of no other way to describe it. She was filled with an inexplicable need, an ache that was growing, and she could not think what it was. But it needed to be sated.

"Yes, best friends," murmured Percy.

Caroline and Jemima had been too old to play with Percy really, and so the four of them—Esther, Lucy, and Sophia—had each created their own call.

And now it was just her. Just her and Percy.

"I…"

"Yes?" Lucy said eagerly.

Percy dropped his gaze. "I…I suppose you should be getting back. To your family, I mean. Now the engagement is announced."

Disappointment dampened the flames of whatever it was within her. Lucy rose to her feet, hating that she was moving away from him, but not knowing what else to do.

"Yes, yes I suppose I should," she said distractedly. "Unless—"

"Yes?" Percy said eagerly, rising to stand beside her.

"Unless you would like to come with me?"

Why was that distress in Percy's eyes? Lucy could not understand it. What more could she say—what more could she offer him?

"No, I think I will let the Fitzroy family celebrate together," said Percy quietly. "Goodbye, Lucy."

"Goodbye," she murmured, stepping away from him before she could say anymore.

Though what was there to say? That she considered him just as much a part of her family as Esther? That the rest of the day would be bereft without him?

That something was happening, changing between them…and she did not understand why she desperately wanted it so much?

CHAPTER FIVE

"W ELL," SAID ARTHUR Fitzroy heavily. "They say all's well that ends well."

There were murmured chuckles around the room, a fire crackling in the blazing fireplace, glasses of sherry in everyone's hands.

Lucy rolled her eyes. *Well, really!* Trust her father to summarize it in such a way; they had never known such riotous excitement in the Fitzroy family in all her years.

Well. Perhaps when Stuart's uncle had died, right there and then while dancing at Caroline's engagement party, revealing Dr. Walsingham was in fact not just a country doctor, but also the heir to the Earldom of Cheshire…

But aside from that…

Selina beamed at Esther, who was sitting rather primly at the end of the sofa nearest the fire. "Well, another daughter married, and to a duke no less!"

"The Duke of Kendal," said Sophia wistfully. She sat in the window as was her custom, but this time, she was not looking out of the glaze but into the room. "You will be the Duchess of Kendal, Esther."

"Goodness, it does not seem entirely right to think of myself in that way," blushed Esther prettily. "I am fortunate the man I have fallen in love with such a man."

Lucy, curled up in an armchair as their Papa strode forward to toast bread on a prong, stared at her sister. In love.

Lucy had attempted to ignore most of it—Christmas Eve had its own traditions, after all, and she had enjoyed losing herself in the familiar customs which appeared every twelvemonth, no matter how many sisters were marrying dukes.

But this year it was impossible to entirely pretend everything was the same. Caroline had stalked away, perhaps a little piqued she now had a sister with a greater title than hers, and Jemima had seemed remarkably quiet. Very concerning for Jemima.

Lucy had sat through hours of countless praise for her soon to be brother-in-law, which was all very well if she had anything to contribute, but most of the Fitzroys barely knew the duke. Some had never even met him.

But there was a dancing delight in Esther's eyes they could not deny. There was no possibility this was a mere dream, a scheme that could disappear before they met at the altar.

No, if there was any reckoning by the way the Duke of Kendal had looked at Esther as he had kissed her hand goodbye after dinner—a look which had fair made Lucy blush and turn away, so intensely romantic had it been—the wedding would need to be swift, and soon.

Lucy attempted to push away the thoughts as conversation about the upcoming nuptials filled the room. It was most scandalous of her to be even thinking of such a thing—and about her sister, too!

No. Young ladies of good family, like herself, do not think about…about that.

Lovemaking.

Lucy shivered as the thought intruded in her mind. She knew the basics of course, had had to be told when she was about to enter Society.

"So, you know what to look out for and avoid," her Mama had said darkly.

As though a gentleman with that sort of thing on his mind could be spotted at twenty paces, Lucy thought with a wry smile.

She had not thought too much about it when Caroline and Jemima had been married; she had been young and not officially in Society.

But she was now, and with Esther about to become a wife, Lucy could not help but wonder…about that side of things.

She swallowed, trying desperately to force away the images rising in her mind, but it was impossible. The shape of a gentleman, a man, holding her close. The feeling of being so held; what was it like?

His hands over hers, fingers intertwining…what would it be like to be close in such a way? She had held hands with Percy, of course, but that was not the same. Not the hot, sparking delight Lucy tried to imagine. Not the same intensity, the same longing, the same need…

A memory of that strange, hot need she had felt a few times the last few days rushed through Lucy and she gasped—though thankfully, her family were too absorbed in Esther to pay any attention.

"—when first I realized he was attempting to woo me," Esther was saying to rapturous exclamations of delight from Sophia and their mother. "And then…"

Lucy smiled, despite herself. It was pleasant to think of another wedding in the family, and hopefully it would distract her from whatever nonsense was taking place in her heart.

In the rush and panic of Esther going missing, then reappearing again betrothed to a duke, Lucy had entirely forgotten to ask Percy what he had meant during their unfinished conversation at the door. She had not chosen a gift for him; there was no point. They had never exchanged gifts. It was one of the things they had agreed on years ago. No gifts, no expectations.

For a heart-stopping moment, Lucy's gaze flickered over to the small pile of wrapped gifts, all ribbons and bows, to the right of the fireplace.

Was it possible Percy had gone against tradition this year and actually purchased a gift for her? Surely not. He would surely know that she had not done so much for him!

Guilt poured into her heart as Lucy considered it, but with a sinking feeling she could think of no other alternative. *Botheration, it was most irritating.* Now he would be waking up on Christmas Day with no present from her after he had gone to the trouble—and it was Christmas Eve today. Tonight. No time to do anything about it.

Lucy sighed heavily. She would have some groveling to do on Boxing Day, she was certain. Percy would certainly not let it lie that she had appeared to forget about him.

"My word, that was a heavy sigh indeed!"

Lucy smiled at her father. "I suppose it was. Did I almost blow out the fire and ruin your toast?"

"Almost," said Arthur, eyes twinkling. "What was all that for?"

"Nothing," Lucy said automatically.

Well, she could hardly explain what had been rushing through her mind, could she? It was hardly the topic for polite conversation in any setting, let alone with her parents.

Lucy swallowed down the bile that rose at the thought. Speak about such things with her parents? *Heaven forbid!*

"Well, I am for bed," yawned her mother, rising slowly and stretching. "It is nigh on an hour past my bedtime, and you know what I get like when overtired."

Her husband caught his daughter's eye and winked. "Couldn't possibly say, my dear."

"You hold your tongue," Selina said good naturedly. "Come on, take me upstairs. Let's leave these young ones to their own devices."

Lucy grinned as her parents left the drawing room arm in arm. It was remarkable—how two people could fall in love all those years ago and still speak and look so affectionately at each other.

Would Esther still look at her duke like that in thirty years?

Would she still have that connection to Percy?

Lucy started, astonished at the thought which meandered into her mind. *Percy?* Why was she thinking about him at that particular moment?

Sophia sighed as she moved from the window sill to the chair their mother had just exited. "It is like a fairytale, Esther, you and the duke. You met, you fell in love, and you immediately became engaged to be married."

Esther smiled a little shyly. "Yes, I suppose it is a little strange."

"I do not think it is strange," replied Sophia, tucking her feet under her and smiling at both her sisters. "I think it's just beautiful, isn't it Lucy?"

Lucy cleared her throat before attempting to speak. "Yes. Yes, very nice."

Well, what was she supposed to say? The Duke of Kendal was not a gentleman she knew. She could not tell whether he was a good man, a kind one, one they would want Esther to be marrying. For all she knew, he was an absolute bore and would make Esther miserable.

He was certainly not the type of gentleman she had imagined for Esther, though now Lucy came to think about it, she was hard pressed to think of anyone in their acquaintance she would consider good enough to marry her sisters.

No one…except Percy.

No. Esther could not have him—Percy was hers, and hers alone.

The thought had simmered before she had even registered it. Lucy glanced at her sisters, chattering away happily about Esther's wedding plans.

Where had that come from? That ferocious anger, that outrage, that jealous feeling that she would never permit anyone to touch Percy?

"Tell us again precisely how it happened," Sophia was saying, leaning forward with wide eyes. "How did you know?"

"Know?" Esther repeated.

Sophia nodded, and Lucy found herself interested, despite herself. "How did you know that you were in love with him?"

"You will have to get accustomed to calling him Jack," said Esther with a laugh.

Sophia's cheeks flushed, and Lucy chuckled at the pair of them.

"The idea of us calling His Grace by his first name is ridiculous, as well you know," Lucy chastised her sister gently.

"Well, what are you going to call him, then?" Esther shot back with a smile. "You cannot exactly call him 'Your Grace' when he is family!"

"I suppose we will call him Kendal, like Cheshire," suggested Sophia, leaning her head against her hand. "How strange it all is, having brothers in the family after so long with just us sisters. I am still getting accustomed to Hugh and Cheshire and Nathaniel."

"And Percy, I suppose."

Lucy looked up, Esther's words gaining her attention. "Percy?"

Esther nodded, pulling her sleeve slightly so it was level with the other. "Yes, he is probably the first brother we ever had, in a way."

Lucy opened her mouth to say Percy was not like a brother at all, then closed her mouth. Their Mama had thought it rather delightful, and their Papa had laughed, and in the end, it was only Lucy who had kept doing it.

But he did not feel like a brother now. Something had changed, something Lucy could not understand, let alone describe to another, but Percy was not the Percy he was before.

"Tell us," said Sophia eagerly. "How did you know you were in love with him?"

Lucy tried to settle herself in the armchair as Esther started to tell the tale. She was getting herself tied in knots, and for nothing, she told herself. The best thing she could do was concentrate on her sister—on her excitement. Try to be happy for her.

"It all started off in rather a strange way, I suppose," Esther admitted, at Sophia's encouraging nod. "I thought I would make him fall in love with me, to show him he could care for me...and it was strange. At first, I thought it was just...well. Like with Percy."

Sophia nodded, as though that particular comment needed no further explanation. Lucy stared between her sisters; what on earth did they mean? *Like what with Percy?*

At the moment, she was not entirely sure whether she knew what it was like with Percy. His presence the last few days had made her feel...different. Hot. Uncomfortable.

"And then..." Esther's gaze became unfocused as her mind drifted to memories which clearly gave her much pleasure. "It was in the small things. I found that any moment with him was far superior to anything I could share with anyone else, merely because of his presence. Do you know what I mean?"

"I do," breathed Sophia with a smile.

Lucy hesitated, then nodded.

Because she did. Well, if that was not a perfect description of what she felt with Percy, then she did not know was—that feeling one was entirely understood, accepted. The knowledge one did not have to describe something in great detail to be believed. That warm, comforting feeling that all was right with the world because that person was there.

"And then...it happened over weeks, gradually, of course, yet so fast," continued Esther, her eyes bright and cheeks pinking. "The more I tried to hold myself back—though I admit I did not try very hard...well...I started to feel..."

Lucy's gaze flickered over to her sister.

"I realized I...well. I desired him," Esther said in a rush. "I wanted to kiss him, wanted it more than anything. That tug in my stomach, that need to lean closer...knowing if I was closer, then everything would be perfect...I cannot put it into words."

"It sounds wonderful," breathed Sophia.

Esther nodded as she laughed, a little shakily. "It feels like loss of control and hunger, and—and what I imagine flying feels like. As though everything about the world is different, better because that person is in it …"

Her voice drifted away, and her gaze dropped to her hands in her lap.

Lucy stared. How was it possible for Esther to describe that odd sensation she had experienced with Percy the last few days?

That warmth, that spreading heat which seemed to come from within her, even though there was no rational explanation for it? That need to be closer, that strange leaning she had experienced. The way her heart had thundered in her chest as her fingers had intertwined with his own...

Lucy swallowed. No. It was not possible. She was not in love with Percy.

"And...and the more I thought about it, the more difficult it became to think of something to get you. I thought...I thought maybe we were planning to...to get each other the same Christmas gift."

No. No! It was impossible. It would make no sense for her feelings to change, for her to fall in love with...with...

"And at the end of the day," Esther said with a small laugh, "I knew life without him, the thought of him with anyone else, married to someone else...it would be intolerable. I would not survive it. And that was when I knew..."

"It was true love," breathed Sophia.

Lucy moved not an inch, as though the simple act of breathing would somehow upset her mind, prevent it from thinking clearly.

If she were thinking clearly, which she was not entirely sure about any longer. How was it possible that she should have fallen in love with Percy—Percy Ardingley!—and not known it? Surely that was ridiculous.

Falling in love with Percy in the first place felt ridiculous!

"I wanted to kiss him, wanted it more than anything. That tug in my stomach, that need to lean closer...knowing if I was closer, then everything would be perfect...I cannot put it into words."

Esther's words echoed in Lucy's mind, muddling her thoughts and constricting her airways.

In love…with Percy? Was that what these new and strange sensations meant? Was she in love?

Lucy had always thought falling in love would be…well, like it was with Esther. Meeting someone, finding a thunderbolt struck you as your eyes met, and that was it. You just knew. You had to be together, had to be close to them, needed to kiss them, and before you knew it, you were engaged.

Not…not like with Percy. A slow, steady trust that had built up over years, a friendship that had blossomed as children and had deepened as adults. A knowledge of the other person that was almost absolute, and a need for them as one would a friend.

Or perhaps, a need that grew. That one did not notice changing, shifting, until all of a sudden it was impossible to ignore.

"I…well, I have wanted to tell you for some time, and there has never been a good moment."

Lucy's stomach turned over. And he had noticed. Of course, Percy had noticed. There was nothing about her that got past him. Even before she had been conscious of it herself, Percy had seen within her these growing buds of desire.

And he wished to stamp them out. *Of course, he did,* Lucy thought frantically, *he had no wish to upset her, to desire to raise hopes that could not be fulfilled.*

No wish to hurt her with his lack of interest.

Understanding, painful and cruel, dawned rapidly now as all the pieces fitted together.

"And…and the more I thought about it, the more difficult it became to think of something to get you. I thought…I thought maybe we were planning to…to get each other the same Christmas gift."

He had not got her a gift—Percy was merely trying to ascertain whether she had bought him a gift, to save her the disappointment of his lack of reciprocal affection.

Oh, it was all so embarrassing. Had she already made a fool of herself?

If Lucy could have done so without attracting the interest and concern of her sisters, she would have dropped her head into her hands. It was all she could do not to rush out of the door.

Well, she was in love with Percy. She loved him, wanted him, desired him, desired his company as well as his kisses. She knew that now.

And she would have to face him on Boxing Day in the full knowledge that her affections for Percy Ardingley were not returned.

CHAPTER SIX

THE MOMENT LUCY opened her eyes the next morning, all the chaos, panic, fear rushed back into her mind and her heart. *She was in love with Percy Ardingley.*

Worse, she was in love with him and had not even realized it until last night. She was in love with him, and he was not in love with her.

The connection they shared, the beauty of the moments they shared…it was all over. They could never return to how they were, not now she had realized just how desperately she needed him.

Lucy stared up at her bedchamber ceiling, the same small crack in the left-hand corner just the same as ever.

And one day Percy Ardingley would meet someone, a lady completely different to her, and fall in love with her. He would marry her and leave Lucy all alone.

Lucy's jaw clenched. *Alone.* Yes, for she could never countenance marrying someone else. Not now she knew what it was to have such a connection as she had with Percy.

Even if it was not reciprocated.

"Wake up!"

A loud banging on her door echoed around the room, and even in the depths of her confusion, Lucy could not help but smile at Sophia's loud exhortation.

"I am awake!" she called without moving.

Well, why should she? Her bed was lovely and warm, and this Christmas Day was absolutely freezing, judging by the cloud of breath that appeared as she called back to her sister.

"Lucy Fitzroy, get out of bed this minute!"

Lucy sighed. That was the trouble with family traditions at Christmas; they absolutely had to be carried out, even if she had no wish to partake in them this year.

A discomforting jolt disturbed her stomach as she pulled her legs over the side of the bed, wincing at the freezing cold air.

This would be the last Christmas she shared with Esther.

Well, not quite, Lucy told herself as she pulled on her underclothes, shivering slightly at their chilly temperature. It was not as though Esther and her duke would never spend Christmas with the Fitzroy family London.

Wasn't it?

Only as Lucy pulled up her favorite Christmas gown, the one with the elegant print of holly which she saved for Advent, had the horrible thought occurred to her.

After all, it was not as though she knew any dukes…but from the little she knew of Caroline and her earl, they had to spend at least two in every three Christmases at his estate, the mansion Lucy had visited a few times and had been in complete awe of.

Would that be the same for Esther—or perhaps more? Would she in fact be forced to spend every Christmas at the Duke of Kendal's residence?

Sadness tinged with a little confusion mingled with happiness for her sister as Lucy finished doing up the buttons on the side of her gown. It was all changing, and not like when Jemima had married or even Arabella. They had married gentlemen, yes, but not with titles that would pull her away from her sisters.

Would they ever have a Fitzroy Christmas again—as they used to?

"Get up, lazy Lucy!" came the cry in the corridor as Sophia banged once again on her door. "If you don't get moving, I'll open all your presents myself!"

"I am almost ready!" called Lucy, though from the clattering noise of someone rushing down the stairs, it did not seem to matter. Sophia had already hurtled to the drawing room.

Lucy shook her head wryly as she pulled the rags from her hair, shook it wildly, then attempted to pin the mass of curls up as swiftly as possible. Really, it made so little sense to curl her hair if she was only going to force it up in pins again.

An image popped into her mind: herself, curls loose, flowing down her neck and shoulders…and Percy before her. Staring at her, an appreciative look on his face. Looking at her as he never had before. The imagined Percy stepped forward, a blazing look in his eyes, his hands reaching for hers—

A crash echoed around the Fitzroy house from downstairs.

"Sophia Fitzroy, be careful!"

Lucy swallowed, pushed away the scandalous thoughts of a Percy who loved her in the way she loved him, and glanced quickly at her reflection in the looking glass. Well, she was presentable at the very least, and that was all that was required on Christmas Day. She would ask her mother to borrow her lady's maid before they started for church.

Before then, however, she had the Fitzroy Christmas traditions to enjoy.

"There you are!" said Esther as Lucy entered the breakfast room. "I have had a fair fight on my hands, trying to keep Sophia away from your gifts!"

Lucy laughed as Sophia opened her mouth in outrage. "You have not! Why, you yourself said that if Lucy did not come down directly, then you would—"

"Peace, girls," interrupted their father.

Lucy sat beside Esther and her mother with a quiet smile.

She would have to force Percy from her mind, that was all. He did not love her, and that hurt—but it would certainly be most foolish of her to dwell on that when there was such a pleasant Christmas Day ahead of her.

If only she could focus on that, instead of the glorious images she was trying not to dwell on…

"Now then, one gift before breakfast, that's the tradition," said Selina with a wry smile. "Which will you choose, Esther?"

"Has the duke given you a present?" asked Sophia eagerly.

"I do not think he has had time to, though his hand is more than enough for me."

Lucy rolled her eyes. *Did Esther have to be so…so sickly sweet?* At least the Duke of Kendal was not here yet, for who knew what he would do in response.

Blow kisses across the breakfast table, no doubt.

Lucy almost laughed at the ridiculous image—but her laughter died away instantly as she imagined Percy blowing kisses at her. Kisses which would land softly on her lips, lips that waited for him to—

This was getting silly. Highly conscious her cheeks must be darkening with heated embarrassment, Lucy attempted to distract herself by reaching for a gift from the small pile.

One was evidently from Jemima, her untidy scrawl on the label; one was wrapped in what appeared to be gold paper, that could only be from Caroline—but this one had no label.

Lucy picked it up. A small rectangular thin box wrapped in brown paper. There was no ribbon, no adornment whatsoever, no label to indicate its giver. She turned it over, in case there was an inscription directly on the brown paper itself underneath, but no. Nothing.

"Who is that from?" asked Esther, pulling brown paper from a gift that looked remarkably like some sort of bird feeder.

"Arabella?" Lucy guessed.

Her sister nodded, then looked at her gift and pulled a face. "I do like our brother-in-law, Nathaniel is very charming…but really. His obsession with birds—"

"With nature," corrected their mother. "Oh, Esther, they are—well!"

Lucy tried to hide a grin as their mother held up the pair of gloves Esther had knitted for her—rather poorly, it had to be admitted, though Selina undoubtedly would rather swallow nails that reveal such an opinion.

"How…how charming," said Arthur helplessly.

Lucy hid a giggle and turned her attention back to the parcel she had picked out. Well, she perhaps would have a clearer idea of who the giver was when she opened it up. Perhaps it was from a Fitzroy cousin. One never knew what state things would be in when they arrived at their final destination, after all.

Pulling off the brown paper, Lucy was none the wiser when a long, thin cardboard box was revealed.

"What is that?" asked Sophia from across the table.

She had opened her gift, it seemed, and was adorned with a pretty scarlet-jeweled bracelet Lucy had not seen before.

"I don't know yet," said Lucy, carefully pulling the top of the box off. "It looks like…"

"A whistle?"

Esther appeared to be correct. At least, Lucy could not think what else it was, a flute, perhaps?

But no, it was too short to be a flute, and the mouthpiece was directly aligned with the two holes further down. Made of carefully whittled wood, the whistle was unpainted and otherwise unadorned, resting on a bed of silk.

Lucy picked it up gingerly, as though it could fall apart when touched, but it appeared to reveal no secrets. There was not even a label or a tag on the inside of the box.

"Who gave you a *whistle*?" asked Esther curiously.

"I…I do not know," said Lucy in wonder.

A whistle? None of her sisters would surely think to give her such a strange thing, and even if they had, they would surely ensure she knew it was their gift, would they not? It made no sense to give a gift without the recipient knowing to whom they were indebted.

If you could call it indebted, Lucy thought wryly. What did she need a whistle for?

"Blow it," suggested Sophia with a grin. "You never know, you could use it to summon Mrs. Castle."

"The day we get a whistle for Mrs. Castle is the day we lose her," said their Mama firmly, with giggles up and down the table. "Do so at your peril."

Lucy could not imagine it was suited for ordering about servants, nor dogs if they had one, but her curiosity was piqued. Bringing the instrument to her lips, she blew.

A low, melodious note emanated from it.

"Pretty," commented her Papa as he glanced at her. "Well made, as far as I can see. What do the different notes sound like?"

Lucy tried putting her fingers first on both the holes, then one.

Phhooeee!

She almost dropped the whistle in amazement. It was their call—her call. Her call with Percy. The similarity was impeccable.

"Goodness, that sounded like—"

"It's your call!" said Esther, interrupting their youngest sister with her eagerness. "Your call with Percy!"

Lucy lowered the whistle, staring at it in wonder. *Was it possible...could it be that Percy had had this made especially for her? A way to sound their call? Was this what he had meant?*

"*And...and the more I thought about it, the more difficult it became to think of something to get you. I thought...I thought maybe we were planning to...to get each other the same Christmas gift.*"

Surely not; there was no possibility Percy had thought Lucy may give him this sort of gift for Christmas! So, what on earth did he mean?

"What a kind boy," said Selina affectionately. "I always said his future bride will have a kind husband."

Lucy almost opened her mouth and spilled her secret, her recent revelation that it was she who had to marry him, must marry him—that she could not endure the thought of anyone else having him!

But she managed to keep her thoughts to herself, and instead just sat in wonder, Percy's whistle between her fingers.

Affection rose in her heart, soaring through her body, and making it impossible to eat, to speak, to think. She cared about him so much, and in a way, it was hard to believe she had only just realized the depths of her affection last night.

Lucy had thought, in that dark moment, that she was alone in this. That Percy did not care for her, that he was merely embarrassed at the change in her. But what if she was wrong?

She twirled the whistle thoughtfully between her fingertips as her family continued to chatter on. What if Percy did feel something for her, something more than she had thought.

"I...well, I have wanted to tell you for some time, and there has never been a good moment."

Fear, excitement, hope, dread, all rose within her. Could it be more? Could Percy have been the gentleman of her heart all this time, without her actually realizing it?

"I...well, I have wanted to tell you for some time, and there has never been a good moment."

If her affection, a feeling Lucy was still trying to understand herself, was in any way reciprocated, she had to know. Waiting until tomorrow was impossible, waiting a single hour was inconceivable.

She had to think of a way to escape her family, at the soonest opportunity.

Phhooeee!

"Lucy, as pretty as that whistle is, I would prefer it if you did not play it at the breakfast table," her mother called down to her.

Lucy blinked. She had not brought the whistle to her lips; it had not been her call.

And that could only mean...

"Yes Mama," she said obediently, rising to her feet. "I will take it upstairs so I am not tempted again."

Lucy could not step outside of the breakfast room fast enough. Heart pounding as she closed the door behind her, she made not for the stairs but for the corridor that led to the back door of the garden.

When she opened it, a beaming Percy was on the doorstep, leaning against the doorframe, a whistle identical to hers in his hands.

"I thought for a moment you had not heard me call," he said with a grin. "Yet here you are, just when I wanted you."

"Just when I wanted you."

Lucy did her best not to melt right then and there in the doorway. How had she never noticed this before? How had she never realized just how wonderful Percy was? How fortunate she was to have him in her life, how she could never be apart from him for more than a few days?

Had she already missed her chance?

"I had to leave my family at the breakfast table," she said a little breathlessly.

Lucy swallowed, trying to force her lungs to cooperate. How was she so dizzy just standing here? How had she never noticed quite how handsome Percy Ardingley was?

Heart thumping wildly, Lucy tried to think, tried to act normally—as though she could recall what normal was.

"I like your gown."

Lucy blinked. "What?"

"Your gown," Percy repeated, his grin becoming a little mischievous. "Goodness, it's like you hardly woke up this morning. What is with you today, Lucy?"

"Nothing," she said quickly, trying to ignore the little twist of pleasure—for she knew what it was now, could not ignore—in her stomach as he said her name. "I just...thank you. For the whistle."

"Our call," Percy said, laughing. "It took me far too long to get it right, but after the first, the second was thankfully far easier."

Lucy stared, then dropped her gaze to the whistle in her hands. Carefully whittled from wood, every inch of it a masterpiece. "Did—did you make these yourself?"

Percy gave her a mock bow. "You would be astonished how difficult it is to find a craftsman who knows your special whistle with your special girl."

There it was again, that twist in her stomach, but it was joined now by a strange ache between Lucy's legs that she had never felt before.

She wanted him. What was it Esther had said?

"But if a gentleman kissed you, Lucy…what would you do?"

Yes, she understood it now. An ache, a need, a want. A feeling one could not live without the other person. The question was, how on earth was she supposed to explain that to Percy?

And what if she was entirely wrong? What if Percy did not care for her in that way, did not return her affection? Was this it, the end of their friendship, for surely it could not be maintained if she revealed her foolish, one-sided love?

"Lucy?"

Lucy's gaze flickered up and saw a concerned look on Percy's face. "I was just thinking…if you created these whistles because you are struggling to do our call now, after so many years. Is that it?"

She tried to inject a little teasing wit into her words, and saw with a lurch in her heart that Percy returned it.

"No, I just thought it was easier this way," he said simply. "After all, I intend to give that call for the rest of my life."

Lucy did not exactly plan it. At least, she had the impulse to do it and she gave into the impulse immediately, but that did not mean she had expected it to be so…so…dramatic.

Four inches higher than Percy, thanks to the step, Lucy leaned forward and with one hand grasped the lapel of his greatcoat.

"Lucy, what—"

Percy had no opportunity to ask anything else—no one could, with someone else's lips on theirs.

Lucy's heart had frozen in her chest as she realized just what she was doing, kissing Percy. *Kissing Percy!*

But the instinct was there, and finally, she knew what it was, giving in immediately, crushing her lips on his as her chest collided with his own, her hand pulling him close.

For an instant, Percy froze, and Lucy froze with him, unsure precisely what was supposed to happen next. Well, it was her first kiss, after all! The warmth of his lips, their softness, called out to her in an aching way, as though she had finally come home, but still Percy did not move.

It may have been a mere second, perhaps a heartbeat.

However long it was, it was too long—but he did not leave her waiting any longer.

In a sudden and swift movement that made Lucy gasp in his mouth, Percy dropped his whistle and pulled her into his arms, his lips crushing hers as his tongue demanded entrance.

And Lucy let him—how could she deny him? She would deny him nothing as her body was sparked with pleasure, pleasure she had never known before, tingling across her body, to the very reaches of her fingertips.

"Lucy," moaned Percy into her mouth as the kiss deepened, taking more from her than she thought possible.

But she gave it willingly. She would give him anything, be anything for him, do anything for him—if it meant having Percy in her life, in her embrace, then nothing was too much nor too little for him.

He was Percy. He was everything. And only now did Lucy luxuriate in the knowledge that he, too, felt something—whether it was love or mere lust, she did not know.

In this moment, it did not matter.

The kiss finally ended, though Lucy remained tight within Percy's embrace. Their chests moved in uneasy rhythms, their breath entirely stolen by the kiss.

For a moment, Lucy was not sure if she could look him in the eyes, so embarrassed by the sudden boldness that had overtaken her and propelled her into his arms...but when she did, she saw to her relief that Percy had a lazy, yet satisfied grin on his face.

"I wondered how long it would take you to work out," he murmured.

Lucy's heart leapt. He loved her—surely that was what he meant! He loved her, and she loved him.

"Oh," was all she could manage.

Percy chuckled, Lucy feeling his laughter as well as hearing it. "Oh Lucy—I wanted to tell you, I have wanted to for so long, but I knew until you were ready, you simply would not—what?"

He halted as Lucy placed a finger on his lips, silencing him.

"You always do interrupt me," he said, his words muffled under her finger.

Lucy rolled her eyes, her breath short and her mind whirling.

She loved him. He loved her. All the years of friendship had not merely been building a foundation of amiability, but something far more…interesting.

Far deeper. More intoxicating. Wilder. Something that called deep within her, something that made Lucy want to something she knew was absolutely out of the question.

It was not the sort of thing ladies did. Certainly not Fitzroys.

"Lucy?"

"Lucy!" called an entirely different voice. "Lucy, we're almost ready for church—where are you?"

Lucy hesitated only for a moment. "I have a headache," she called over her shoulder. "You go, I will stay here. Do not disturb me when you get back, I will likely be asleep."

Jumbled sorrow came about her headache, advice on taking a little linctus, and a promise not to disturb her after church, all echoing down the passageway.

Lucy did not care. She was not listening. She had turned back to Percy, who had a puzzled look across that handsome brow she knew so well.

"Lucy?"

"Now we have finally found each other," Lucy whispered, hardly believing she was about to suggest such a thing, "why don't you come inside?"

There was still nothing but confusion on Percy's face. "But you have a headache."

Lucy rolled her eyes. He really was the dearest man she had ever met, but sometimes…

"Percy," she said slowly, fixing her eyes on his. "I have sent away my family. We are alone here. And I am inviting you inside."

CHAPTER SEVEN

L UCY'S HEART BEAT so fast, so loudly, she was certain Percy would be able to hear it. But did that matter? Did he understand her now—what she wanted, what she craved? What she was certain only he could give her?

"Percy. I have sent away my family. We are alone here. And I am inviting you inside."

She looked up into his eyes, wide and astonished, yet with none of the distaste Lucy had expected. Well, it was not every day a woman of good standing and reputation invited in a gentleman for…well.

Though she had not spoken the words, she was certain Percy understood her.

She wanted him. Wanted him in her bed. Wanted more than that, more than they had shared, more than what she knew, for Lucy was certain there was more.

Percy swallowed hard. "You may not understand quite what you are—"

"I understand perfectly," interrupted Lucy.

"You interrupted me again!"

"Only because you were speaking nonsense," Lucy said with a smile. Could he not see how serious she was, how she knew what risk she was taking? "Percy, I want—I want you."

Percy opened his mouth to speak, closed it again, then said

quietly, "Lucy, I never thought you and I would ever—I believed my feelings to be entirely one sided, never dreaming that you could—"

"Well, I could." Lucy almost laughed, it seemed so ridiculous. Had any woman been forced to argue with a gentleman she wanted to make love to? "Percy Ardingley, if you do not come inside—I-I am…I am aching for you."

In the end, it was the simplicity of her words that appeared to have the greatest effect. Percy groaned, his eyelashes fluttering before he got a hold of himself, leaning one hand against the door frame.

"We have known each other for so long," Percy whispered.

His eyes glittered with unsaid words, words Lucy was only now just starting to understand. Because they had known each other so long, hadn't they? All her life, there Percy had been, right beside her.

Everything was better when he was there, no day as good as when he could be in it.

And she had never investigated those feelings, that flutter of excitement as she knew he would be joining them, that twisting soaring joy in her heart when she was close to him. Had never considered it could be…

"It was always you, Lucy," Percy breathed, his eyes not leaving hers. "Always you, I knew you would realize that, eventually."

"Eventually," Lucy said wryly, her body tingling with anticipation, though for what, she did not know. "Damn, Percy, why didn't you ever say anything?"

"I tried!" he said with a dry laugh. "But you know how hard it is to get a word in edgewise with you, Lucy."

"I know nothing of the sort," she said softly, desperate to reach out for him again, knowing she could not, should not, yet this need was building within her.

"I am not sure if you know what you do to me."

"I would like to find out," said Lucy.

She was unable to continue. Percy had stepped forward, forcing her to take a step backward into the house, but that was not what she cared about. No, she was far more focused on the lips that had crushed against hers, filled with passion and desire as she had never known.

Lucy gasped in his mouth, causing if anything only more passion to rain down on her lips, Percy's hands on her waist pulling her closer, the intensity of his presence, his smell, the way he held her close, utterly causing all sense to be forced from Lucy's mind.

If only she could live here forever, in the closeness …

Percy pulled away, looking down into her face with wild eyes. "You know there is no going back, after this. No taking back what we do, no restoration of your…"

"Innocence," breathed Lucy.

She knew, it just as she knew the sea was wet and the wind was cold and the stars shone brightly for lovers like them. They belonged together.

But what did she care? Though her reputation may be ruined, though her innocence would be gone, it would be given to the one man in the world whom she knew would take good care of it.

Besides, it was not as though this would be the one and only time they would ever…ever be together. This was it, the rest of their lives. Lucy knew that once they shared this most intimate of things, they would never be able to leave each other.

Instinct told her that. At least, she thought it was instinct. Instinct or a call to her very core that she could not ignore.

"Come on," she breathed.

Percy had never been upstairs at the Fitzroy house. Had never needed to; all their socializing had been downstairs, or outside, as was proper. Nothing about this was proper.

Pushing him before her, Lucy giggled as they half stumbled, half ran up the stairs. Percy had reached the landing and had turned back to look at her when Lucy froze.

"Lucy? Lucy, are you sure you wouldn't rather one of us stay home with you?"

Lucy swallowed and turned on the stairs to look down at Esther, a well-meaning smile on her face along with a concerned frown.

"Headaches are most horrible things, after all," her sister said, shaking her head. "I could stay behind and—"

"No," Lucy said swiftly, then seeing the startled look of hurt on Esther's face, "I mean, no, thank you."

Had Esther seen Percy? From what Lucy could tell, he was just far up enough along the landing to be invisible to prying eyes…but if her sister took a step forward…

"Please, I just need to go to bed," Lucy called down. "Honest—you go, have a wonderful time."

When Esther sighed, nodded, and walked along the hall, shutting the door quietly behind her, Lucy sagged against the banister.

"I thought she would never leave," came Percy's voice above her. Lucy looked up and saw him grin. "Now, you were heading to bed, which I think a very fine idea indeed."

Lucy shivered. This was certainly not the sort of thing she could ever have imagined before, but with Percy, it felt right. Perfect. *Overdue.*

It took just a few steps up to reach the landing. Percy was waiting for her there, breathing heavily, though it could not be from exertion.

He leaned forward, and Lucy eagerly closed the gap, bringing her mouth up to his to be kissed, her entire body quivering alive as their lips met. Oh, this was heavenly, Percy's hands on her waist, that strange tug within her drawing them close, closer, closer…

"So," Percy breathed, breaking the kiss just long enough to speak. "Which is your bedchamber?"

Lucy swallowed. This was it. The point of no return …

"This one," she said softly.

Unsure precisely how they had managed to get in there, Lucy closed the door behind her and leaned against it. Percy stood in the center of the room, glancing around, and she was suddenly conscious of just how intimate this was.

Not just the lovemaking, though she was certain that would be far more intimate than she could have imagined.

But no, having him here at all. In her bedchamber. A place where no man, save her Papa, had ever stepped. All of herself was on display here—her favorite books, the gown she had summarily thrown into a chair last night, the tray of hair pins on the toilette alongside her best ribbons...

The parts of her no one else saw.

"I have never done this before," Lucy blurted.

Percy turned and raised an eyebrow, his handsome face now covered in mischief. "What, invited a stranger to your bedchamber?"

She had to laugh at that. "You are no stranger, Percy."

"You are no stranger, Percy."

And she was right. Percy Ardingley was no stranger to her; in fact, there were few people who were as close to her as he was. A man she trusted, a man she adored.

A man she loved.

There was no one else in the world, Lucy knew, she would rather share this with. No one else she could even consider to be a part of her life as Percy was. Whenever he called, she answered. Whenever she called, he was there.

He was all she wanted.

"Lucy?" Percy's expression of mischief had disappeared, replaced with concern.

Lucy smiled and stepped forward, taking his hands in hers. "I trust you, Percy. I want this, and I need you to be sure that—"

"More sure," said Percy, his voice low and dark, "than I have ever been of anything. I told you before, Lucy. I have wanted this for...wanted you for far longer than you could imagine."

Their kiss was soft at first, sweet. Exploratory as their lips parted and the kiss deepened, drawing them closer together, Lucy's fingers entangled in his hair,) and Percy's hand clasped around her waist.

But as the kiss deepened, so did their desperation to be close. His fingers trailed down her waist to her buttocks, and Lucy gasped in his mouth as he pulled her closer, tighter to him. It was wonderful, this sense of closeness, togetherness—and instead of the awkwardness and uncertainty Lucy had assumed would be a part of her first lovemaking, the rare times she had ever thought of it, there was nothing but comfort and sizzling desire.

She wanted Percy.

"Oh, Lucy," Percy groaned, removing his lips from hers.

Lucy moaned at the lack of contact, pulling him closer, desperately trying to kiss him again—but her moan became a gasp as Percy obeyed her cry but in a most unexpected way.

Instead of kissing her on the mouth, his kisses trailed down her neck and to her décolletage. Quivers of pleasure soared through Lucy, a desperate sense that this was where he belonged.

Kissing all of her.

It was all she could do to stay upright, her legs shaking as the intensity of Percy's attentions rushed through her, but his strong hands cupping her buttocks kept her balanced.

"Percy," she breathed.

It was all she could manage.

Percy's kisses were dancing across the tops of her breasts, and Lucy was overcome with the desire for more. There must be more; there would surely be greater heights of pleasure they could reach, together, if they could simply remove these clothes.

"Take off my gown," she breathed.

Percy halted his kisses immediately, straightening up to look into Lucy's eyes. "Are you—"

"Stop asking me if I am sure," said Lucy, a half-smile teasing across her lips. "And don't complain that I've interrupted you again! I want you, Percy Ardingley. Show me how much you want me."

It appeared he did not need much of an invitation. A growl in his throat, Percy's fingers moved swiftly to the buttons of her gown, and Lucy gasped as he pulled them apart, forcing the gown to slip to the floor.

The raw demonstration of his desire for her was intoxicating, desperately heightening her own sensations—and she knew precisely how to respond.

In a few quick movements, Lucy reached out and tugged Percy's coat from his shoulders. The clothing fell to the floor, but she was prevented from doing anything next as Percy dipped his head to remove his boots. Only when he straightened up did Lucy pull out his shirt from his breeches and wrenched the shirt up over his head.

Oh, dear Lord. Lucy had known in theory, naturally, what a gentleman had underneath his clothes—but she could never have predicted just how delightfully handsome Percy Ardingley was. How had she managed to miss him all these years? How many ladies had looked at her, eyes full of jealousy, as a man like this stood by her side?

"You are…beautiful," she murmured.

There were no other words for it, at least, none others that she could conceive of.

Percy's eyes glittered as he took her in. "Beautiful…beautiful is not the word."

A flush tinged Lucy's cheeks as she looked at herself, her undershift still covering her modesty but only just. This was not how she had expected to first reveal herself to a man…but could there be a better man to share this with?

"You first," she said, shyness overcoming her.

Percy caught her gaze, and for a moment, Lucy was certain she had seen just a hint of nervousness in his own expression. Of course, this was all new to him as well; she could see that in the way he held himself.

Which made this all the more special. Neither of them had done this before…it was all new.

Hesitating only for a moment, Percy slowly undid the buttons of his breeches without taking his eyes from Lucy, and then let them fall to the floor.

Lucy gasped. Well, there he was…all of him. His manhood erect, twitching slightly, as though desperate for her touch. Which it probably was.

How she longed to reach out, touch that soft skin, see what reaction she inspired, for Lucy was certain it would bring them closer as nothing else ever had.

"N-Now you," Percy breathed.

Well, she could hardly do anything else now he had revealed himself to her—but Lucy found, to her surprise, that most of her fear had faded away. This was something they would treasure forever. There was no need to hide, not anymore.

Answering his call, Lucy slowly lifted her fingers to the ties of her undershift, lifted them from her shoulders, and pulled them out. She watched, delight soaring through her heart, at the growing attraction in Percy's eyes as she teased him.

He groaned. "Don't keep me in suspense, Lucy, please!"

His manhood twitched again, and Lucy felt a surge of pleasure in this strange control she had over him.

Slowly, without taking her eyes from him, Lucy let the material slip, ever so softly, through her fingers.

Percy moaned as he took in the sight of her. "Damn, Lucy…"

She worked hard not to cover herself with her hands. Percy had stood before her, open and naked, and she owed him that same treat.

By the looks of it, she had a marked effect on him—but she had no more time to attempt to take it in. Percy stepped toward her, pulling her into his arms, and Lucy gasped at the sudden intensity of his skin against hers.

"Percy—"

He claimed her lips as she was about to ask him to do just that. Shivers of pleasure rushed through Lucy as her breasts pressed up against Percy's chest, his hands on her waist now far more intimate than before.

"Do you trust me?"

Lucy blinked, sight hazy, as Percy pulled away from her just a few inches and looked searchingly into her eyes. "Trust you?"

He nodded. "There is something I have always…for years, I have wanted to…but it is…unusual."

Gaze sharpening, Lucy frowned, though her heart was racing, intrigue at this unusual request he wished to make of her.

"I promise," Percy said, kissing her neck and making her quiver, "you will enjoy it."

Well, with such a promise, how could she say no? Lucy nodded, a smile on her lips.

Percy groaned, pulling her to the bed. "Do as I say, but if you wish to stop, just say."

Lucy stepped forward, hardly knowing what to think, only how she felt—and that was that she wanted more of this pleasure, more of this touching, more of this closeness that only grew the longer she was with him.

Percy. The man she loved.

Love. It was a strange word, one she had never ascribed to a gentleman before. But what else could this be?

He was lying on the bed now, his head on her pillow, but before Lucy could ask what it was that he wanted, Percy pulled the pillow out from his head and threw it onto the floor.

"Come here."

Rather awkwardly, Lucy clambered onto the bed alongside Percy—but he smiled, and shook his head.

"No, I want you to…Lucy, I want you to kneel over my face."

Lucy flushed. Surely he could not mean—but it appeared he did.

A delicious hunger was across Percy's expression, and he nodded encouragingly. "I want to kiss you, kiss you and lick you and taste you, between your legs. Oh, please, Lucy…"

There was such longing in his voice that something throbbed between Lucy's legs. Well, what harm could it do? It would not hurt her, of that she was sure.

Nervous, Lucy moved to straddle Percy's chest and slowly, trying not to think about how intimate this moment was, she held onto the headboard and crept up his body until she was right over his face.

"I don't know why you would want to—Percy!"

Lucy almost collapsed with the intense sensation of his tongue licking her secret place, exquisite pleasure shooting through her body.

This was too much, surely it was too much—how was she supposed to kneel here with his mouth doing...doing...

"Lucy, you taste incredible," Percy whispered before licking her once more. "Oh, Lucy..."

Lucy closed her eyes, the overwhelming pleasure rippling through her body as Percy halted speaking but started doing something far more enjoyable with his mouth. Sucking, licking, teasing, twisting his tongue against her, then darting in...

Her fingers clenched the headboard as her head tipped back, too much pleasure to keep herself still.

"Oh, Percy, more, yes," she moaned, hips shaking, unable to help herself, relieved that all her family and the servants would be at church. "Yes, yes!"

Something was building inside her, building so deep and dark she could not understand it, but Lucy knew it would lead only to greater heights of pleasure, and so she held herself there, Percy's tongue licking her to more and more pleasure, until—

"Percy!" she cried.

The crest of pleasure suddenly overwhelmed her, making her body shudder and shake, ecstasy soaring through her in waves, again, and again, and Percy did not cease his kissing and licking until Lucy cried out his name once more, then slipped to the side, her arms and legs quivering, utterly lost to the sensations.

Percy held her softly, and when she opened her eyes, grinned. "Christ, I have wanted to do that to you for so long—you tasted even better than I thought."

Lucy had no words. This lovemaking business, it was far more than she could ever have hoped for. "But you—you have had no pleasure."

Percy chuckled softly. "You think that gave me no pleasure?"

Before she could answer, he pulled her down the bed and onto her back. Looking up at him, Lucy smiled. Everything about what they had shared was perfect, but she had a feeling there was more perfection yet to come.

"Ready?" Percy breathed.

Lucy nodded, unsure precisely what he could possibly mean, but then she arched her back in unexpected pleasure.

Percy had gently nestled himself between her legs and slid his manhood within her, still slick from his kisses. "Oh, Lucy…"

She quite agreed. Having Percy inside her…feeling herself stretch to accommodate him, feeling every twitch of his manhood, the glorious sensation of him within her…

He captured her mouth with his, and Lucy eagerly gave herself up to the kiss, and just as his tongue met hers, Percy lifted himself up and thrust into her again.

"Percy!" Lucy broke the kiss and stared up at him, and Percy for the first time since they had entered her bedchamber looked a little abashed.

"You wish for me to stop?"

Lucy took in a shuddering breath. "I never want you to stop. Harder. Faster."

A look of surprise and delight crossed Percy's face, and he was as good as his word.

"Lucy!" Percy cried out in desperation. "Lucy!"

"Yes!" Lucy gasped as he tipped her once more over that crest, her whole body shaking as the peak of pleasure overwhelmed her. "Percy!"

Perhaps it was the way her body moved, perhaps it was her cry, she was not sure—but Percy thrust suddenly, jerkily, within her and collapsed into her arms.

There they laid together, wrapped in each other's arms as the waves of pleasure slowed and subsided. Lucy's eyes were still closed, but she did not need to see to know she had finally found her home in Percy Ardingley's arms.

CHAPTER EIGHT

LUCY WOKE UP reaching for him.

Percy. It was natural after what they had shared, vague memories shifting through Lucy's memory as she slowly moved from sleep to wakefulness. After all, had he not been by her side for hours—almost the entire day. Her family's lack of return had not worried her; she'd had more than enough to keep her occupied.

Lucy blinked in the darkness. It must be late afternoon. She turned to look at the empty place in the bed beside her and smiled. Percy.

What they had shared, what they had done to each other. Touching, kissing, stroking, teasing…it had all been so wonderful. More than she could have hoped for, certainly more than she had ever expected.

Half-forgotten desires she had pushed aside had been brought to the tip of her tongue. Nothing she had suggested had been ignored by Percy, and she in her turn had tried out some of the desires of Percy's heart.

It was difficult to tell, precisely, which she had enjoyed the most.

Lucy sighed and sank deeply into her pillow, pulling the bed-clothes up to her chin. It was marvelous, it was wild, it was impossible, it was scandalous…

And all with the one man she had had by her side for so long, and never really noticed.

"Lucy, I never thought you and I would ever—I believed my feelings to be entirely one sided, never dreaming that you could—"

Lucy swallowed. It was impossible to believe she had not seen Percy in that way for so long—but now she had, it was impossible to see him in any other.

"This is so special, I hope you know that," Percy had whispered as they had drifted off to sleep in each other's arms, their naked bodies pressed against each other, their pleasures taken, exhausted, panting, spent. "So special."

He had kissed her then, gently, brushing his lips against hers, and Lucy had closed her eyes, lost in the perfection of the moment…and fallen asleep.

It must be…what, late afternoon? Early evening?

Lucy glanced over at the clock on her toilette table. Just gone a quarter past five. Why, she and Percy had spent the entire day enjoying each other.

Noise below echoed around the house and gentle laughter drifted in under her door.

Lucy sat bolt upright. Yes, they had spent most of the day enjoying themselves—and had fallen asleep before the family had returned. They had obviously been detained at church, likely as not invited back to the vicarage for luncheon and carols.

And that meant they had left her up here, thinking she was sleeping off a headache when they had returned…

Lucy stifled a laugh. Well, it was rather amusing. What on earth would her family say if they knew precisely what kind of Christmas gift she had received this year!

Thinking of Christmas gifts, Percy's whistle soared back into her mind, and then of course the gift giver. Lucy looked around the dark bedchamber; Percy's clothes, previously abandoned on the floor, were gone.

Percy was gone.

The thought darkened her heart, filling her chest with panic.

Percy was gone, the man she loved, the man she had shared so much with. Where was he? Why had he gone, and without saying a word to her, either?

There would be a reasonable explanation for this, surely. He would have left a note. The question is, where would it be?

The obvious place would have been her toilette table, but there was nothing there. Nor was there a note under her pillow. Try as she might, nowhere Lucy looked could she see a note.

A strange, unsettled feeling moved into her stomach.

No note? Why on earth would Percy leave without a note?

Discomfort crept across her body as Lucy sat on the end of her bed. It could not be…no. Percy would not betray her in that way. He would not take from her all he could, make declarations of affection, share with her the first moments of exquisite pleasure…then merely abandon her.

He would not. He could not. That was not the man he was. The man she knew.

Lucy swallowed, tasting bitterness in her mouth. She was overthinking this. Surely Percy would return.

Then something caught her eye, and she rose swiftly, stepping across the room to a chair where she had carelessly left yesterday's gown. Upon it lay…a pair of whistles.

Lucy blinked. Her whistle…and Percy's. Both of them. He had left his whistle here.

Red hot confusion rushed through her bones. What did that mean—that he was not going to call on her again? Whatever this was, whatever lust-fueled moment this was for Percy, it would not be repeated?

After all, though he had spoken of desire, had he ever spoken of affection? Of…of love?

"No, I want you to…Lucy, I want you to kneel over my face."

It was enough to make her nauseous, but Lucy swallowed down the bile. She had to ensure her family never knew of this. She would not permit them to know just what a foolish woman she had been, how easily she had lost her virtue. How they had perhaps all been taken in by Percy Ardingley.

It took but a few minutes for her to dress and pull a shawl around her shoulders and creep out of her bedchamber. As she shut the door behind her, Lucy could hear the excited joyful laughter of her family downstairs.

Snippets of their words crept up to the landing.

"—tell you again, that's cheating!"

"Who decides the rules here?"

"I say, no need for a fight to the death!"

More laughter, more joy. Lucy's heart twisted painfully. Perhaps, in time, she could attempt to speak to Esther about it all...

She opened the drawing room door.

A magnificent sight met her eyes. Her entire family—well, almost all of it—were in two halves; her sisters Caroline, Jemima, Esther, and Sophia on one side, all seated and looking up at their parents, Stuart and Hugh, who were acting out some sort of charade. The Duke of Kendal appeared to be adjudicating, a broad smile on his face.

"Lucy!" Esther beamed, patting the place on the sofa beside her. "We wondered whether we would see you today—how is the headache?"

"Headache?" repeated Lucy stupidly as she stepped over to join her sister.

"Headache," said Caroline smartly. "You said you had a headache, that is why you did not accompany us to church."

"And a wise choice indeed, for we ended up at the vicarage tasting the most disgusting mulled wine, I tell you now," Jemima said, making a face.

The whole room laughed, and Lucy smiled weakly. "Oh. Headache."

Of course, that had been her excuse not to attend church with her family—her way of getting Percy on her own.

"Headache?" repeated Stuart with a frown. "Have you had headaches often, Lucy? You really must—"

"No more of your doctoring tonight, are we playing charades or not?" asked the Duke of Kendal briskly, a teasing grin on his face. "I believe you were about to start?"

"And no speaking this time!" Sophia said, pointing a finger at their father. "I am watching you, Papa!"

Their father made a face, and all the Fitzroy sisters giggled. Lucy sank into the seat beside Esther and tried to smile.

Her family. Life continued, it seemed, whether she had betrayed herself, whether she and Percy had done something wild and radical or not. It was strange to see them all so happy, so content, Caroline and Jemima arguing over their guess, and Hugh attempting not to giggle.

As though nothing had happened.

"Do you not think him a remarkably handsome man?"

Lucy blinked. "What?"

She turned to Esther, unsure precisely how her sister had managed to discern what she was thinking. It was most irregular for anyone to know what she thought of Percy! After all, she had only just started to understand herself and what she thought of Percy, and the idea of discussing it…

"Jack," said Esther. "The Duke of Kendal, I suppose I should call him in company, but family does not count as company. Is he not handsome?"

Oh, of course. Esther was talking about her betrothed. Lucy looked for a moment at the duke, who was trying to shout down a debate about the rules with Stuart, and shrugged.

Well, he was a reasonably proportioned man, she would give him that; but there was none of the spark and catalyst Percy had. The way he held himself…

Now she came to think about it, had Lucy not always compared gentlemen to Percy? None of them had attracted her attention or caught her eye, but was that because perfection had already been seen?

"Yes," Lucy said quietly. "Very handsome."

Esther beamed. There was a strange sort of glow about her,

something Lucy had never seen in her before, but it did not appear she was needed much in the conversation.

"I cannot believe sometimes I have been so fortunate as to attract someone as handsome—but of course, Jack is far more than handsome. He is the Duke of Kendal, yes, but he is more than a title...I cannot tell you, Lucy, just what he means to me..."

Lucy nodded as Esther prattled on, clearly not needed to contribute anything for the conversation. Her sister had more than enough to say about her future husband.

"—the way he looks at me, sometimes I cannot believe..."

Lucy swallowed. She had felt that way only a few hours ago. Percy had looked at her as though...well, as though she was the most beautiful woman in the world. As though it would be impossible for him to look that way with another.

"—and the more I think of it, the more I realize that truly it was a Christmas miracle," sighed Esther happily. "I cannot imagine being happier than I am, and in a way, isn't it marvelous that we can all share in my happiness? Are you not happy, Lucy?"

"No," Lucy said without thinking.

A frown appeared on her sister's face, and Lucy saw all too late a small shake of the head from their youngest sister, Sophia, seated just along from them in an armchair.

"No?" repeated Esther, confusion in her voice. "What do you mean, no? Aren't you happy for me?"

"I just...I need your advice," said Lucy in a low voice.

There was no one else in the family she could speak to. Esther was the sister closest to her in age, the natural peacekeeper. She was always looking for a way to bring people together, to reconcile them...perhaps she would be able to advise her on Percy? On why he had suddenly disappeared from her side?

"Oh, I am not sure there is much I can advise you on, I will be busy planning the wedding," said Esther with a laugh. She smiled at her intended, and the Duke of Kendal broke off his debate with Stuart to return the smile. "Yes, the wedding will have to be remarkably different from what I had thought. I suppose Caroline may be able to help, she is a countess now after all, but—"

"I know you have a wedding to plan, but you do not need to make those preparations right now," cut in Lucy, a prickle of irritation across her heart. "I just…I have a dilemma."

Esther beamed. "Oh, when it comes to dilemmas, I am the best. Why, when Jack said—"

"Esther," interrupted Lucy.

Her sister blinked. "What?"

"I was trying to tell you about the problem I have," Lucy said, trying not to become irritated. Her nerves were stretched as never before.

Would the world ever feel the same again? Now she had found herself in this…well, entanglement with Percy, for want of a better word, would she ever find any equilibrium?

A knowing and rather irritating smile slowly crept across Esther's face. "Ah. Yes, I thought you may ask me about this, and it is absolutely simple."

Lucy blinked. "It is?"

The situation with Percy was many things, she would give her that—but simple? That was certainly not a word she would have used.

Esther nodded, patting her hand gently with that same knowing look. "Yes, and you need not concern yourself. I have already sorted it out."

Lucy's eyes widened. Surely that was not possible—but then, Percy may have run into the family as he left. Perhaps he had seen Esther—perhaps he had already explained himself to her!

Hope soared in her heart, dissolving all her fear, her frustrations, her concerns. There was an explanation, a reason why he had disappeared, and now Esther could put her mind at ease.

"Yes, it was relatively easy, really," said Esther with a beaming smile. "With only two sisters left unmarried—save for myself of course, but not for long!—the decision was easy. I will have yourself and Sophia as my bridesmaids."

Lucy sagged as cheers went up on the other side of the room.

Evidently the charade had been deciphered. "Esther, that is not what I meant! I mean—"

"Well, what else is there?"

"Not everything is about you," Lucy snapped, unable to help herself.

Esther's face fell.

Well, it was the truth! Here she was, her heart broken and innocence gone. Surely Esther should be able to see that in her face—yet all her sister could do was go on and on about her precious duke!

For some reason, the room was silent. Everyone was looking at her, surprise on her brothers-in-law's faces and shock on her mother's.

Lucy swallowed. *Ah.* It appeared she had been a little louder than she had intended.

Well, it was not as though she had said something that was not true, had she?

"I see," Esther said coldly. "So, what you mean is, it can't be about me?"

Without waiting for an answer, she rose from the sofa. After muttering something in the Duke of Kendal's ear, the two of them stepped silently out of the room.

The door closed with a snap.

Lucy swallowed, regret seeping into her heart, mingled with defiance. She had not said anything she would not say again. Probably.

"That was not very kind," Sophia said quietly.

Lucy's stomach twisted painfully as the truth of her sister's words settled in her chest like a lead weight. "I know."

There was no point in denying it. She could see the truth of it in the disappointed faces all around the room.

Agony at Percy's absence, desperation to understand just what she had done, and shame at the way she had responded to Esther all mingled within her, overpowering her reason.

It was all too much. How was it possible to suffer this

much…and at Christmas?

She had given her innocence to Percy, and he had not only taken it, but then discarded her immediately afterward as though…as though it was nothing. As though she was nothing.

Lucy swallowed. It was certainly not the Christmas she had expected.

The evening did not continue much after that. Charades was abandoned, a few leftovers from the seemingly sumptuous dinner were enjoyed, but all the joy of the evening had gone. Before Lucy knew it, everyone had traipsed up to bed, and she went to her own bedchamber alone, empty and cold as it had never been before.

The night was long, and by the time Lucy surfaced and came downstairs for breakfast, it was with a genuine headache as regret pulsed through her veins.

Regret at what she had said to Esther. Regret at the way she had lied about her headache the day before. And most of all, regret about Percy.

Lucy pushed him from her mind as she sat silently at the crowded breakfast table. She would not think of him. She would not give him any chance to overtake her mind.

"Post," said her mother with a too bright smile. "One addressed to all of us, shall I open it?"

Murmured assent echoed around the table. Lucy smiled weakly as she helped herself to toast and started buttering it. Both Jemima and Caroline looked a little worse for wear after yesterday evening's celebrations.

Selina opened up the letter, and beamed. "It's from Harmony! At least, I think it is…goodness, where are my spectacles? Her handwriting is so small…Lucy dear, will you be so good as to read it?"

Lucy had no time to agree or decline, the letter already placed in her hands. Looking down, she saw Harmony's handwriting was indeed tiny, thin compressed lines that darted back and forth over the paper.

"How is she?" asked Esther stiffly.

Lucy glanced at her sister further down the table, but Esther did not meet her eyes. She had not yet, it seemed, forgiven her. "Quite well, as far as I can see…talk about their Christmas preparations, a concert or two in Bath…"

And I suppose the real reason for writing, dear cousins, is that there is news from us I simply cannot keep to myself any longer. We were not sure for a long time, but our doctor has confirmed it. I am with child!

She dropped the letter in her shock, and all eyes turned to her.

"What is it, Lucy?" asked Sophia urgently. "There is no bad news?"

"Bad news…nothing of the kind!" said Lucy, hardly able to believe she had been the first to know. "Harmony says she is going to have a baby!"

Cries of delight echoed around the table, and Lucy smiled. It was good news. Harmony had been married for four years now and would make a wonderful mother. In a way, it was surprising they had not received such news before.

Jemima burst into tears.

The table fell into instant silence, surprise on each face as Hugh brought his arms around his wife and pulled her into his chest.

Lucy stared, dropping the letter to the table, then glanced at Esther who seemed similarly astonished. *Jemima…crying?* Their sister was not one to express emotions at all, other than irritation, and to burst into tears right at the breakfast table…it was unheard of!

"Jemima?" said their father weakly.

"She is quite well," said Hugh hastily as his wife sobbed into his chest. "I think I will take her—"

"It's not fair!" wailed Jemima, genuine distress in her voice. "A-Are we never to have a child?"

Lucy's heart sank. She should have realized. Jemima and Hugh had wed within a few weeks of Harmony and David, and neither couple had welcomed any children to the world in the four intervening years.

Jemima's face, red and blotchy, turned to her husband as her tears overcame her.

"Now, then," said Hugh quietly. "What have I said, a thousand times?"

Jemima gulped, brushing away her tears as she said quietly, "That you married me for me, not for the children I might give you."

"And I meant it then, and I mean it now," Hugh said fiercely, so much that Lucy felt embarrassed to be hearing such words of tenderness between a husband and wife. "I love you for you, Jemima, and if we never have any children, I will still be the most fortunate man in the world. And you know that."

Jemima nodded, snuffling slightly as she remained tight in his embrace.

Lucy's heart stirred, not just in sympathy for her half-sister, but as understanding soared into her mind.

The love and affection shown by her brother-in-law…it was mirrored in her own heart, for Percy. She loved him. His sudden absence from her side after they had shared something so deep, so personal…was it possible that he did care for her, and she was right now missing the opportunity to be held by Percy just as Jemima was held by Hugh?

Lucy stood up so hurriedly that her knife clattered off her plate to the table.

"Lucy?" Esther said, eyebrow raised.

"I need to—I will explain later," she said in a rush, almost running from the table.

"But Lucy, where are you going?" came the cry from her Papa as she reached the door.

Hand on the handle, Lucy turned with a smile to look at her family, hope now pulsing in her chest. "I am sorry to leave you all so suddenly, and on Boxing Day, too—but I have to make a call."

CHAPTER NINE

LUCY'S HEART BEAT frantically as she rushed down the London streets still coated with Christmas snow. What she was planning…well, it was foolish. Ridiculous.

She was going to make a complete idiot of herself and all before Percy, the one person she never thought she would be embarrassed in front of in her life.

But she had to. As Lucy turned a corner and was forced to halt before crossing the street as a pair of carriages rushed past, Lucy knew there was no possibility of her staying at home rather than going to Percy's house.

She had to say how she truly felt about him; regret would always be her companion if she did not try to understand what on earth had happened between them.

Lucy's pulse was thundering in her ears by the time she reached Percy's street, and a little of her confidence disappeared as she saw cheerful candlelight streaming from the houses.

Everyone was awakening to Boxing Day, a day to sit and eat leftovers and chatter merrily with loved ones. And here she was, rushing away from her family to speak to a man who…

Well. Had certainly seen more of her than she had ever believed possible. A man she loved. A man who had always answered her call, who had always been there for her, who had been the companion she had never known she had needed.

Lucy's fingers tightened around the whistle she had grabbed from her bedchamber just before she had thrown on a pelisse and rushed out of the house.

Did she dare? Even after coming all this way, was she ready to have a conversation about their friendship—their love—that had lasted almost all her life?

Her feet halted just outside Percy's home. There was a holly wreath on the front door, covered in red berries and a gold ribbon. Lucy swallowed. This was it. She needed to make a decision, choose whether to risk love and affection...or call the whole thing off.

Phhooeee!

The whistle recreated their call perfectly, so piercingly loud Lucy wondered if the whole street would come out to see what the noise was...but Percy's front door stayed shut.

Heart in her throat, Lucy waited for what felt like an eternity. Two heartbeats, twenty...and yet still nothing. He did not want to answer her call. He did not want her.

Turning away, tears sparkling in her eyes making it difficult to see, Lucy tried to step forward, but her legs did not seem to want to move. It was impossible to see, her ears roaring with her pulse, and—

"Lucy!"

A voice as dear to her as her own made Lucy stop. Blinking away the tears threatening to fall, she looked up at the front door. It was open. In the doorway was a gentleman, napkin still tucked into his cravat, eyes wide.

Percy. Percy Ardingley.

With a rush of relief, Lucy swallowed down all the words that rushed to the tip of her tongue. That she loved him. That she missed him.

That she could not understand why he had just disappeared like that, abandoned her, disappeared off into the evening air with no more than his whistle.

That what they had shared, though beautiful, could not be

repeated because she could not bear to be left like that again.

"Percy," Lucy said in a cracked voice. "I—"

"Oh, thank goodness, I thought I had lost that," Percy said with a wry smile, shaking his head as he pulled his napkin off and dropped it on a console table just inside the door. "Thank you."

Lucy stared. Lost that? Lost her, he meant? How on earth did he not realize that by leaving her without a single word, she would not know if he truly wished to marry her?

Then she looked at where his gaze was pointed, and realized her misunderstanding.

The whistle. He was looking at the whistle in her hands; he thought she was merely here to return it to him.

"Come on, pass it over," Percy said easily, extending his hand.

Lucy swallowed. Yes, it would be a simple exchange; she would leave him the whistle, and her heart, and then she would return home. She had been a complete fool to think she would have the gumption to say anything to him after what they had shared.

Heat blossomed in her cheeks at the remembrance of just what they had shared. So much, such pleasure…and she would never feel that again.

The idea of sharing it with someone who was not Percy—no. It would be impossible.

"Lucy?" Percy said, his hand falling to his side. "Are you well? I am sorry to have left my whistle with you, I did not intend to."

He did not intend to?

Lucy stared, struggling to take it all in. "Percy," she said firmly, rather astonished at how strong her voice was. "We need to talk."

Percy's eyebrows rose. "Goodness. Should I be concerned?"

It was a good question, though not one she could answer. Lucy's legs trembled as she walked forward to the steps up to Percy's home, and he stepped aside to let her in. This place was just as familiar to her as her own home was. Why, she had spent so many hours here it was almost a home away from home.

Now it would be the scene of the most important conversation in her life.

"Breakfast room is a state, there is no point going in there," Percy said breezily, closing the front door behind her. "Drawing room, I think, is best."

Lucy nodded, saying nothing as she entered the suggested room and laid the whistle down on a table. *There.* Now even if she had to rush out of the place in tears, she would at least know she had delivered Percy what he needed.

The man threw himself onto a sofa and beamed up at her, as though nothing at all had occurred between them the previous day.

"Well?" he said calmly. "You said we needed to talk."

Lucy nodded, hands shaking as she clasped them before her. Percy had not invited her to sit down, but they had never waited on ceremony like that before. They had never needed to.

She sat slowly on a sofa opposite him, moving a red velvet cushion and hugging it into her stomach as though it were a shield.

If she did not speak soon, she would not be able to speak at all, and this entire visit would all be for naught. She just had to say what was on her heart.

"Percy," Lucy began seriously, not quite meeting his eyes.

"Lucy," he said with a teasing grin. "Goodness, I have never known you to be this serious. Everything—everything is well, I trust, with your family?"

There was a note of fear in his voice, and Lucy tried to smile. "All is well. Well, not entirely well. Jemima was sobbing when I left, and Harmony—"

"Jemima was sobbing—*Jemima?*" repeated Percy, and Lucy finally had enough courage to look at him. A perplexed look was on his face. "Are you sure you do not mean Caroline?"

Lucy had to laugh. Caroline would be mortified to know it, but she did have the reputation of the six Fitzroy sisters as being the one most likely to cry...at anything.

"No, it was definitely Jemima," she said wryly. "I believe it was mostly sorted by the time I...Hugh was comforting her, and Harmony's news was not intended to harm—"

"Harmony's news?" Now Percy was leaning forward, real concern in his eyes. "What's wrong with her?"

"Nothing," Lucy said hastily. She had not intended to regale Percy with all the Fitzroy news, she had come here for one purpose only—and if she did not speak soon, she would lose all courage. "She is with child, but—"

"Oh, that is excellent news! Harmony has wished for a child for years, or at least, I thought she had," Percy said, not permitting Lucy to get a word in edgeways. "You all must be thrilled— except for...Jemima. Ah. I see."

Lucy nodded. That was the trouble with families, wasn't it? The celebration of one could bring tears to another, even if there was no intention to injure. *Those we love*, she thought, *are the best at hurting us.*

"I suppose, if we are in the same boat, we will have to be careful around Jemima, too," said Percy thoughtfully. "Hmm. I had not thought of that."

Lucy stared at the man before her. *What on earth was he talking about?*

Percy was now looking at her as if she was just as odd as he was being. "Well, if Jemima gets that upset with the news of your cousin being with child..."

He trailed off delicately, as though what he was saying was perfectly reasonable.

Only then did understanding dawn. Lucy's face flushed red hot, and she was certain her hair was matching her cheeks as the realization of what Percy was saying sank in.

Of course...they had taken little precaution yesterday, thinking only of pleasure and their desire to be close. There was a possibility, however faint, that yesterday they had...and she might...

"Look," she said decidedly. "I know we made no promises to

each other, no commitments—and I am sure you will wish to know in the coming weeks whether we are…"

The thought stilled her tongue. *With child—with Percy's child? It was a heady thought.*

"You made no demands of me, and I exacted no promises of you," Lucy continued, her voice faltering. "Our friendship is—was—so important to me, Percy, the last thing I would ever wish to do is ruin it, and I cannot help but feel I have…or at least, we have. I am not explaining myself properly."

"That you certainly are not," said Percy slowly, a frown appearing. "Lucy—"

"You should know that I care about you a-a great deal," said Lucy, cutting across him and looking down once again at her hands. *She could do this. She could.* "A great deal."

"Lucy—"

"Even if you do not care for me in…in that way," Lucy continued, mercilessly, forcing herself to look at Percy's crestfallen face, "Enough to marry me I mean, I thought it important to try to…well. Keep our friendship alive. I want to, I mean."

"And so do I," said Percy softly.

Silence fell in the drawing room, and Lucy tried not to let her disappointment show.

Well, she had made her grand speech, hadn't she? At least, as best as she could make it—and Percy had said naught but that he wished to keep their friendship.

No big speech of affection from him, no declarations of love, no wild promises he certainly would never keep. He did not even attempt to pretend he was in love with her.

If only she had not fallen in love with him, Lucy thought wretchedly. If only she did not care for him so. If only her entire life had not been entwined with his, for entangling him from her affections would be troublesome indeed.

For some strange reason, however, though disappointment sank into her stomach like a lead weight, Percy appeared to be quite content. In fact, he was smiling.

"What?" Lucy said defensively.

Percy shook his head as he chuckled. "Lucy Fitzroy, you are the most inexplicable—"

"Percy!"

"Will you let me get a word in and stop interrupting me?"

"Never," said Lucy decidedly as she rose to her feet. *Well, there was no point in staying here any longer, was there? Not if she was to be insulted and laughed at for pouring out her heart!* "I wish you good day, sir."

She had almost managed to take three steps across the room before a hand, strong and warm, grasped hers.

"You do know I am terribly, foolishly in love with you, don't you?"

Lucy stared. Had those words really come out of Percy Ardingley's mouth?

Percy laughed, pulling her into his arms. "Lucy Fitzroy, do you mean to tell me you didn't know?"

"How one earth could I know?" Lucy spluttered. *Percy loved her?*

"You do know I am terribly, foolishly in love with you, don't you?"

It was not possible. It was impossible!

"I did not think it needed to be said!" said Percy, his lips brushing against her forehead as his hands pulled her tightly into his chest. "What else did you think I meant when I said yesterday how I had waited for years for you to realize, how I had hoped you would see it, how I had waited for you! Damnit, Lucy, we don't have to say everything aloud between us for the other to know!"

"B-But…"

"I would have thought my actions yesterday would speak more than enough about my devotion and attraction to you," he said more seriously. "You think I would do such things on a passing fancy?"

Lucy's cheeks reddened even further, she was sure of it, even as her heart soared and joy, finally, started to outweigh disbelief.

"And I would like to point out," said Percy with a teasing laugh, "that at this point, I am the only one of us who has made declarations of affection!"

"That is not—I told you yesterday!" Lucy protested, a wry smile teasing across her lips as the reality of her situation started to feel real.

She loved him—and he loved her. They loved each other. It was everything she could have wanted, and more.

Percy was shaking his head. "Not quite, and not enough! Come on, I need to hear it. How much do you adore me?"

Lucy thumped him heartily on the chest. "Less and less the more you tease me, you brute!"

She may have said more, she was not entirely sure, but she was given no opportunity to. Percy's hungry lips met hers, and Lucy gave herself up to the kiss, the delighted relief that they were together and would never be apart.

The kiss deepened, Percy bestowing pleasure on her lips, and Lucy moaned, parting them to let him in, knowing what heights of ecstasy the two of them could reach.

"Damn, woman," breathed Percy heavily. "I did not think I would be up to the challenge of ravishing you again so soon, but the things you do to me…"

"Don't just talk about it," Lucy said, hardly knowing what she was saying as the words poured from a deep, dark part of her. "Show me."

Hazy desire clouded Percy's vision for a moment before he said, "Just to be completely clear, for I would hate for there to be any further misunderstandings. You are marrying me, aren't you?"

Lucy's heart soared. "Of course. You think anyone else would have you?"

"I'll punish you for that," growled the man she loved, lifting her bodily from the ground and walking her, protesting, to the hall.

"Percy Ardingley, what do you think you are doing!"

"Lucy Fitzroy, I am doing what I should have done years ago," said Percy firmly, ignoring Lucy's giggling squirms as he started up the staircase. "When I first realized your call did something to me that no other did—I am bedding you, good and proper, in the bedchamber that will soon be ours!"

Lucy stared as they reached the landing. "You are?"

"I am indeed," Percy said grinning, lowering his head to tease his lips tantalizingly over hers. "And the next time you call my name, I want to hear you beg."

About Emily E K Murdoch

If you love falling in love, then you've come to the right place.

I am a historian and writer and have a varied career to date: from examining medieval manuscripts to designing museum exhibitions, to working as a researcher for the BBC to working for the National Trust.

My books range from England 1050 to Texas 1848, and I can't wait for you to fall in love with my heroes and heroines!

Follow me on twitter and instagram @emilyekmurdoch, find me on facebook at facebook.com/theemilyekmurdoch, and read my blog at www.emilyekmurdoch.com.